child of dandelions

"A beautiful, touching story of a child caught between two worlds, in a country caught in the grip of a brutal army dictator. Shenaaz Nanji evokes wonderfully the purity and bewilderment of a child awakening to terror and discovering a wretched reality."

—M. G. Vassanji, two-time Giller Prize winner

"This is a gripping tale full of beauty and horror, friendship and betrayal, family and country, love and fear. It opened up a whole new world to me, peopled with rich, believable characters. Nanji never lets up on the tension inherent in the story. Historical writing at its best."

—Carol Matas, award-winning children's author

"Drawn in part from the veteran author's own experiences, this deeply felt tale takes readers to 1972 Uganda ... Readers will feel her inner conflict sharply, admire her resilience and quick thinking—and come away shocked themselves by the brutality she encounters during this little-known historical episode."

—Kirkus Reviews

child of dandelions

Shenaaz Nanji

Second Story Press

Library and Archives Canada Cataloguing in Publication

Nanji, Shenaaz
Child of dandelions / by Shenaaz G. Nanji.

ISBN 978-1-897187-50-0

1. Amin, Idi, 1925-2003—Juvenile fiction. 2. East Indians—Uganda—Juvenile
fiction. 3. Ethnic relations—Juvenile fiction. 4. Family—Uganda—Juvenile fiction.
5. Forced migration—Uganda—Juvenile fiction. I. Title.

PS8577.A573.C44 2008   jC813'.54   C2008-903918-1

Printed and bound in Canada
Printed on recycled paper

Second Story Press gratefully acknowledges the support of the
Ontario Arts Council and the Canada Council for the Arts for our publishing program.
We acknowledge the financial support of the Government of Canada through the
Book Publishing Industry Development Program.

 ONTARIO ARTS COUNCIL
CONSEIL DES ARTS DE L'ONTARIO

 Canada Council   Conseil des Arts
for the Arts   du Canada

Published by
SECOND STORY PRESS
20 Maud Street, Suite 401
Toronto, Ontario, Canada
M5V 2M5
www.secondstorypress.ca

With love to my family
and to the children of refugee families

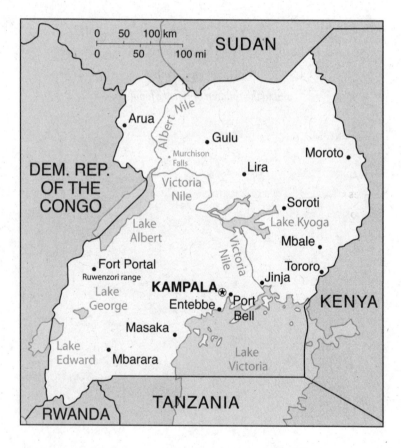

— Author's Note —

Throughout history, cultures have suffered when poverty, prejudice, and intolerance have created breeding grounds for hatred and violence. This novel explores the consequences of such injustice and inequality on two friends and their communities.

—Shenaaz Nanji

── The Dream ──

The river of jubilant people alarmed Sabine as they bobbed along Allidina Visram Street in Kampala. What was the event? she wondered. Not Independence Day. Anniversary of the military coup? No. Then what?

The August sun forced sweat down her forehead and along her neck. The road sweated, too; the melting tarmac oozed sticky black streaks. Sabine and her best friend were winding in and out of the spice-scented alleys of Little India when they ran into the parade.

The dark faces drew closer. Women in bright *gomesi* and headscarves danced, and bare-chested men punched their fists into the air, chanting, "*Muhindi, nenda nyumbani!* Indian, go home."

Sabine felt she was drowning in their cries.

Her friend Zenabu pressed her arm. "They mean British Indians, not you."

Sabine nodded, ignoring the burn inside her. She was born here. Her father was born here. They were Ugandans. Other Indians, like their neighbour Lalita, were British.

Scores of people thronged to cheer the demonstrators. They stood atop boxes, on cars, and on rooftops, waving fronds of the *matoke*, plantain, trees. The girls found themselves engulfed in the crowd jostling elbow to elbow in the heat. A bystander jabbed a finger into Sabine's back. "*Eti, muhindi,* go back to India!"

Sabine turned around to see who had spoken, and spit grazed her chin.

She wiped off the insult, biting the inside of her cheek and restraining her tears. The man could not tell that she was Ugandan. *I wish I were dark like Zena.*

Zena glared at the man. "She's my best friend."

The man laughed. "One day you'll see with new eyes." He picked up a rock by the footpath and flung it across the street. *Crash!* The display window of Sari Fashion shattered, and shards of glass scattered on the road like a broken diamond necklace.

Sabine spotted an army truck in the corner of the alley standing idly by as the crowd cheered and chanted, "Down with *muhindi dukawallas!* Down with the shopkeepers!"

Flying stones, crates, cans, and street debris hit the windows of other Indian stores. People ran carrying radios, cash registers, and even sewing machines. Sabine and Zena rushed past the torrent of bodies, colliding with hands and legs, tripping over a headless mannequin wrapped in a sari, scrambling again, running, running, running.

Safely home in the comfort of the sitting room, Sabine heard on the radio that President Idi Amin had had a dream. In the dream God told him to expel all foreign Indians from Uganda. The newsman said, "Hundreds danced on the streets to celebrate the President's dream."

Celebrate? How silly thought Sabine. Clearly, it was a riot.

"Nonsense!" Papa laughed his conch-shell laugh, and her little brother echoed it.

Mama's betel-brown eyes grew bigger. "Sadru, we are Indians."

"Ugandans," Sabine corrected, looking at Papa, who nodded.

"In fact, we are even more Ugandan than the ethnic Africans. Not only were we born here, but we *chose* to be Ugandan citizens when other Indians remained British." Papa turned to Mama. He put his hand on her lap. "Don't worry, Guli. We may be a handful of golden raisins among eleven million, but we control Uganda's economy. You can't bite the hand that feeds you."

Before Mama could respond, the newsman on the radio said, "All foreign Indians will be weeded out of Uganda in ninety days. Today is day one of the countdown."

Sabine looked at Papa in confusion. Had the President's dream become law?

— The Goat —

Sabine swung her satchel over her shoulder and climbed into the front seat of Uncle's red Alfa Romeo. She could hardly wait to see Zena. Today they would trade costumes and practise a dance they were going to perform at the President's banquet on Independence Day, October 9. But first she freed herself from her tight black shoes. Then she peeled off the milky white socks that her mother insisted she wear. She stuffed the hated shoes and socks into her satchel and found her sandals, the ones like Zena's.

Sabine bent down to strap them on. She wished Papa were home. He had left on a business trip. The hourly countdown on the radio about the expulsion of foreign Indians had turned her mother into a bundle of raw nerves. Mama wasn't going to let her go to Zena's today because Mama's left eye was twitching, a bad-luck sign.

"That's an old wives' tale," Sabine had said. "Wake up, Mama. This is 1972!"

Sundays belonged to Sabine. On Sundays she flew wild and free with Zena. And during school holidays the girls met at her grandfather's Kasenda farm, at the foot of the mist-laden Ruwenzori Mountains in Fort Portal. Bapa called the girls "twin beans of one coffee flower."

Thankfully, Uncle had shown up at a perfect time and offered to drive her. Sabine knew that Mama would not be able to refuse her own brother. From the car, Sabine saw Uncle's broad back as he tried to pacify Mama on the doorstep, her bony hands squeezing together as if she were kneading roti. Strange how her feelings for her mother swung between love and hate so quickly, Sabine thought. She leaned forward and cranked up the radio.

"My Bina!" Uncle got into the car, a lollipop stick hanging out of his mouth.

He was Sabine's best and fattest uncle, and he always sucked lollipops. His name was Zulfiqar, but she had called him Uncle Lollipop since she was little.

Uncle eyed her sandals and punched her arm playfully. "I thought Cinderella's shoes changed into glass slippers."

She wiggled the lollipop stick in his mouth. "Not the African Cinderella."

Uncle laughed, pushing back his glasses, lenses thick as stone. "Bina, my Bina," he sang, drawing closer till their foreheads knocked. "What will become of you?"

Uncle was always there for her when her father left on business trips. He came to her dance recitals. He took her to James Bond movies, and even fishing, though they had yet to catch a fish. Recently he had taught her to drive, a secret that only Bapa and Zena knew.

"Let's go, Uncle. Fire up your jet."

The engine revved and the muffler roared as the car shot out of the driveway. Uncle, a safari race driver, spent most of his life looking under the hoods of cars, tinkering with screws and wires to power them up. Soft melodies played on the Hindi radio station as villas with red-tiled roofs and golf-green lawns flew past the window. Sabine was a songbird flying over the purple blossoms of the jacaranda trees.

Sabine's favourite song from the Hindi movie *Aradhana* played on the car radio, and her mind automatically translated the lyrics into English: *When will the queen of my dreams come?*

The king of Sabine's dreams was Zena's older brother, Ssekore. Sabine recalled the feeling of his warm breath brushing her left earlobe. "A beautiful day with a beautiful girl," he had whispered into her ear at Bapa's farm, last holiday. They sat near each other on the hilltop and he showed her how to use his slingshot. The rock hit the tree and he looked into her eyes and drew near as if to kiss her, but how could he? He was Bapa's farmhand.

The newsman cut the song short. "Today is day eight. Eighty-two days remain for foreign Indians to leave Uganda."

"Stupid!" said Sabine, angry at the interruption of her song. She reached out to turn down the volume on the car radio.

They crossed the busy Kampala Road, flanked by banks and hotels, and approached the rough section of town near Nakivubo market, famous for *nyama-choma*, barbecued meat. Ahead, the traffic was chaotic, as a horde of *boda-boda* bicycle taxis swarmed like bees and wound narrowly between cars and buses. Scores of pedestrians toddled along on the footpath, and bare-chested hawkers hauled the long handles of wooden carts filled with goods for barter. Laughter and chatter flowed, so different from the silence and sterility of her suburb of Nakasero.

A taxi followed so close behind them that Sabine could see the driver singing and bopping his head to the beat of the African music blaring from his car radio. Ahead, the scorching tarmac shimmered like a watery mirage. Her head jerked back against the headrest as their car lurched to a sudden stop.

"Sorry, dear." Uncle pointed to a stray goat on the road. "Our new traffic police."

Sabine laughed. An unwritten traffic law in Uganda was to let the goats pass.

The goat, in no big rush to move, whisked its stubby tail back and forth.

The taxi behind them stopped as well. A few bystanders on the road tried to shoo the goat off the road, but it refused to budge. Soon the traffic came to a standstill and the air was filled with the sound of idling engines and the stink of petrol fumes.

The car radio issued advertisements in English with a thick Hindi accent. "Visit Bismillah Butchery for fresh halal meat." Sabine rolled down her window. Off the road to her left lay the lush savannah valley scattered with umbrella-shaped acacia trees. To her right, a string of mud-and-thatch kiosks displayed pyramids of tropical fruits: mangoes, guavas, passionfruit, papayas, and green plantain, matoke, the staple of Ugandans.

The radio buzzed on. "Looking for a gift for that special person in your life?" Pause. "Go to Gold Bazaar."

Barefoot children, *totos*, baskets of fruit atop their heads, ran to Sabine's window shouting in a mix of English and Swahili, "*Tamu, tamu*, sweet, sweet with Vitamin Z," while a man ran to Uncle's window carrying squawking chickens hanging by their legs.

A fast-moving military jeep from the opposite direction stole the show when it screeched to a stop barely a couple of metres away. Now the goat was wedged between the jeep and Uncle's car. Some hawkers, presumably those without a permit, fled the scene; others simply stared.

A tall soldier leapt out of the jeep. He wore a camouflage uniform, its peaked cap perched rakishly on his head. In his hand he carried a rifle big enough to kill an elephant.

Sabine gripped the cushion of her seat.

The soldier strode briskly toward the goat, rifle in one hand, the other clenched into a tight fist. His strong jaw reminded Sabine of Spearman, the African superhero.

He looked at the bystanders. "Whose goat is this?"

The bystanders looked at each other. The silence was palpable. The goat began to prance around in circles.

The soldier cocked his rifle and positioned the butt against his shoulder. Sabine held her breath.

Bang! The shot echoed through the seven hills of Kampala.

Sabine buried her face in her arms, her scream drowned in other screams.

"Bina, Bina, are you okay?" Uncle's hand rested on her back.

Sabine managed a nod and sat up. She could see Uncle's stubby fingers stroking her cheek, but she did not feel anything.

Outside, she saw people gawking at the remains of the goat in a red pool. She saw its hoofed legs splayed at odd angles. She also saw its face, the glassy eyes staring back at her. The goat's midsection was gone. An odour of charred flesh and gunpowder hung in the air. She felt sick. *I will never eat nyama-choma again.*

Her eyes sought the soldier. He stood in his uniform, waving a victory sign to his colleagues in the military jeep. They cheered, "*Uhuru, Uhuru,*" the cry of freedom.

Beep! Beep! Beeeep!

Sabine sprang up in her seat and turned around to see who had honked. The taxi driver behind them looked irritated. Ahead, the soldier's face twisted into fury, and he began to advance toward them.

Sabine stiffened.

"Down, Bina!" Uncle pressed her shoulder, and she slid down until she was squatting on the floor of the car like a roosting hen.

"*Eti! Muhindi,* showing off, *eti!*" The steel nose of the rifle poked through Uncle's car window and grew longer. "*Toka nje!* Out!"

The car door opened. Sabine stared in horror as Uncle stepped out.

It's a mistake. Uncle didn't honk. She rose, stretching only high enough to see out the window.

"You know me? I'm Butabika!" The soldier hit Uncle with the rifle butt, and his glasses flew off.

Stop! Sabine looked desperately at the bystanders outside. Surely they'd help. But they stood as still as the dead goat.

The soldier kicked Uncle, and he staggered and fell on the road. "Go to India! Go back to where you came from."

Pain knifed through Sabine. She tried to rise, but her feet held fast to the floor of the car. What could she do to help Uncle?

Two discordant voices clashed in her mind. Mama's: *If you see a fire, do you put your hands in it?* Papa's: *My boy, if we act like mice, the cat will eat us.*

Papa thought of her as his boy, and always called her his "brave boy."

She poked her head out the window. "Excuse me," she said to get the soldier's attention. "Excuse me," she repeated, a little louder.

The soldier whipped around, surprised to see her. Seven bootsteps, and his face was inches away from hers. His left cheek had three parallel scars, one short, two long.

He grinned at her through her car window. "Yes, Indian Princess?"

Sabine's throat closed. Her lips moved wordlessly. She pointed to Uncle crawling and groping the pavement in search of his glasses. He was totally blind without them. When the soldier turned to see Uncle, she saw the emblem of a gazelle on his sleeve.

The steel nose of the rifle poked through her window. "Speak up," said the soldier, raising her chin with the bayonet.

Sabine remained still as a rock, taking in the acrid smell of gunpowder from the freshly fired rifle. Would he blast her like the goat? Did it hurt to die? Surely he wouldn't kill her. She was only fifteen. "Uncle didn't honk," she said, careful, very careful not to move as long as she felt the steel blaster under her chin.

"Eti, is that so?"

"Officer, it came from there." A stooped old man pointed his stick at the taxi.

"Tuh!" The soldier lowered his rifle and strode toward the taxi.

The old man's grit infused Sabine. She darted out of the car, hurried past the goat—a black halo of flies now buzzed over it—and ran to Uncle crawling on the road, his blue shirttail hanging out of his pants.

She helped him to his feet. He had a red goose egg on his forehead where he had been hit. He looked relieved to see her. He must have missed her exchange with the soldier. She picked up his glasses and put them on for him. Seeing the soldier engaged with the taxi driver, she and Uncle scrambled to their car.

Inside, Uncle drew Sabine closer, one hand on her arm and the other grasping the steering wheel tightly. They watched the soldier through the rearview mirror of their car.

"One-eleven." Uncle ran three fingers on his cheek.

The scars, thought Sabine. The short scar depicted

the number "I," the long scars, the number "II." She¹ nodded.

"Colonel Butabika, butcher of Naguru Barracks," he whispered.

Sweat beaded on Sabine's lip, yet she shivered. She saw Butabika yank the taxi driver out of the car and drag him like a sack of plantain. As the soldier pulled the man past Uncle's car, she saw the driver clearly, the whites of his eyes whiter than his teeth. Then Uncle pushed her down again.

She dropped onto the floor of the car as a sad old Hindi song came on the radio.

Bang!

Sabine felt a trickle between her legs and clenched her muscles. She heard a car screech away as doors slammed and engines revved.

"He's gone. Sit tight, Bina. I'm going to fly." Uncle stepped on the accelerator.

Sabine stayed rooted in her roosting posture, her sweat-soaked blouse clinging to her like a second skin. She did not rise even when they stopped at the flashing neon sign of Zully Motors, Uncle's car shop.

"Bina." Uncle offered a hand to hoist her up.

She caught his cold hand but did not rise. "What happened?" she asked in a small voice, holding her breath, the whites of the taxi driver's eyes still writhing in her mind.

"Bah! Butabika fired over his head to scare him."

Sabine exhaled. She looked down to check her pants. Tiny blot. Her hand gripped Uncle's as she sat up and quickly crossed her legs.

Uncle put his arms around her. "Sorry, Bina. I'm afraid your mama's right. My red babe attracts bulls." He tapped at the steering wheel of his car.

"Uncle," she said, and a tear slipped out before she could stop it. She wiped it off surreptitiously, pretending to scratch an itch near her eye. "He could have killed you."

"Nah, I know the kingfishes of Kampala. I'll nail that savage. The fool will run naked to his granny's grave." He paused. "I'd better take you home."

"No, Uncle. I'm fine." She forced a smile. She wanted to see Zena now more than ever, share with her this terrifying experience.

Uncle hesitated. "Okay, but not a word about this to Mama." They slapped their hands to seal their secret, and he got out to make a quick call at his shop.

Sabine locked the car doors and looked out. Little India was quiet. Sari Silks, Bangle Bazaar, Sudan Store, Bismillah Butchery—all were closed; brass dead-bolt padlocks hung on iron-grille screens. Glass fragments, ripped boxes, and newspaper scraps from last week's riot still littered the roadside. This hour had been the longest in her life, she thought. She looked down and to her horror saw her hands twisting together in her lap just like her mother's. She hated that! She didn't want to be soft and yielding like Mama.

As a young girl in the India-Pakistan war Mama had glimpsed the face of death. One night a gang of Hindu thugs brandishing knives had broken into her family's flat in Gujarat. They ignored the women—Mama, her sisters,

and baby Zully in a smock, whom they mistook for a girl—
but they stripped Mama's father and three brothers to check
if they were circumcised, a sign that they were Muslims,
and then stabbed them to death.

"Today is day eight ..."

Sabine jerked. It was the countdown on the car radio.
Tabla drum beats pounded in her ears. *Dham dham dham.*
"Go home," rang the chanting of last week's parade. "Go
home," said the man who spit on her at the riot. "Go to
India," said Butabika. The *go-go-go* beats pulsed with the
thudding of her heart.

She pulled her hands apart and sat on them. This was
her home. Papa, a respected businessman, exported coffee,
tea, and sugar from Bapa's farms. Bapa had faced the man-
eating lions during the building of the Kenya-Uganda
Railway. He was called Simba. *Mwena simba ni simba,* Sabine
reminded herself—the child of a lion is a lion. Her resolve
steeled. *I will be brave and resilient like Bapa and Papa. I will stand up
against the soldiers.*

She reached out and turned off the radio. But her
mother's frantic voice rushed to fill the void. *Sadru, the dream
has curdled our future, and even all the sugar from Bapa's plantations cannot
sweeten it.*

What if Mama was right?

Sabine's tongue moved around her parched mouth.
Fear had left a sharp, metallic taste. Her insides twisted.
She felt sick. She fumbled for the handle and jerked open
the car door. She leaned over and emptied her stomach.

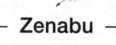

— Zenabu —

Sabine gripped the edge of the seat in Uncle's car, her gaze pinned on the road, as they headed to Old Kampala. They stopped at the red light. She looked right. No military jeeps in sight. Left. None. The road was crowded with pedestrians, cyclists among the few cars. Why did it take so long to get to Zena's today?

At last, rows of white tenement flats came into view, and Sabine began to breathe easier. Each two-storey block, identified by a letter of the alphabet, was divided into eight flats, numbered one to eight. Uncle pulled up near a dense patch of plantain and papaya trees that edged the flats.

Sabine pecked Uncle's cheek. "See you at noon," she said, and got out of the car with her satchel.

Her legs trembled as she made her way to the flats. They were so close to each other that they looked like white squares stitched into a quilt. Zena and Ssekore had moved in here with their Uncle Asafa to attend school after their mother died and their father abandoned them. During school holidays they worked at Bapa's farm and stayed with their Aunty Halima, the farm manager. Sabine always went, too.

She turned in at the last row of flats toward Block H

and across the communal cement compound shared by the tenants of the ground floor; those who lived on the second storey shared the roof terrace. She ducked under the sisal clothesline that stretched from one papaya tree to another.

Zena leaned on her twig broom at the doorstep of their flat, her hair swept into a hundred beaded braids. "What took you so long? I...." She stopped. "What's wrong?"

Clutching the satchel to her thudding chest, Sabine's eyes welled as she told how a stray goat had stopped the traffic and about Butabika and his big rifle. She pressed her lips together to keep them from quivering. "He ... he could have killed Uncle."

Whap! Zena's broom fell, startling Sabine.

"Sorry," said Zena, and they hugged each other.

Zena led Sabine inside the flat. The kitchen was small but bright. A transistor radio played African music. Sabine's nose tickled at the smell of the DDT insecticide.

Zena pulled out a cane-backed chair for Sabine. "I'll make some ginger tea to soothe you—it works wonders, you'll see." Zena filled a pot with filtered water from an earthenware jug and added the tea leaves, ginger, and sugar.

"I hate soldiers," said Sabine.

Zena looked up with her glossy blackberry eyes. "Not all of them are like Butabika. Uncle's a fine soldier."

"Of course," said Sabine quickly. Her toes scrunched in embarrassment and a sandal slipped off. The cement floor was cold and hard. She retrieved her sandal. Zena's uncle, Captain Asafa, was the reason they had the opportunity to perform their dance at the President's banquet.

Zena knelt on the floor to light the Primus stove. "Don't worry. Dada Amin will restore law and order." She looked adoringly at the wall poster of the President. "He's my hero."

Sabine nodded. She wondered what the President was really like. Papa called him *njingo*, an idiot, and laughed at his foolishness; Katana, their servant, feared him, saying he ate the heart of his enemies; the radio and television fondly called him Big Daddy. She looked at the poster of the grinning President. He looked like a friendly giant to her.

Soon the kitchen filled up with the scent of ginger. Zena poured a mug of steaming tea for her. "Here. Drink it hot."

"Thanks." Sabine took the warm tin mug, but her shaky fingers could not grip the handle. She wrapped both hands around the mug and sipped quietly.

The tangy tea trickled down her throat and radiated warmth inside her, and the thudding in her chest slowed. She set the empty mug on the stool.

Zena pressed her hand on Sabine's knee. "How do you feel?"

"Much better, thank you." Sabine forced a smile. She didn't want to spoil her friend's day. "Want to dance?"

They went to the bedroom Zena shared with Ssekore. The only other room in the flat was Uncle Asafa's.

Sabine took her outfit from her satchel. "My *lehnga*. It's a little big for me."

Zena ran her hands over the red silk skirt and blouse and began to change into them at once. Hundreds of round mirrors on the blouse sparkled like moons, and the long skirt trailed on the floor. Sabine helped drape the shimmering *dupatta* over Zena's shoulders. The long scarf fell to her feet like the gossamer wings of a butterfly.

"I look like a memsahib!" Zena spun, and the red skirt flared like a hibiscus in bloom. "They say," she said, her eyes closed, "that if you wear someone else's clothes you get their life."

Sabine nodded. She had heard that saying too. Zena's family scrimped and scraped to make ends meet. Last year, her uncle had borrowed money from Papa to pay Zena's school fees.

Zena reached onto a shelf and handed her gown to Sabine. "My *gomesi*," she said, her voice a little insecure.

"It's beautiful!" said Sabine, reading the Swahili text on the border of the gown. *Dua la kuku halimpati mwewe*. A chicken's prayer will not keep away the hawk. The bright colours of the *kanga* cloth in Zena's gown would liven up Sabine's pale chickpea skin. Mama didn't let her play in the sun, as fair skin was valued in their Indian culture. She began to change, glad to get rid of her pants.

The soft cotton gown pressed against Sabine's breasts, which poked out like small lemons. She was a late bloomer, the last girl in her class to get her period. The long gown flounced and flared over her angular body, and when she walked, it swept the floor like a bride's dress.

"Sabine, you look as pretty as Chief Wangari's daughter!"

Sabine blushed. She wished Ssekore could see her. She took out her portable tape deck from her satchel and played her favourite song. Both Zena and she loved music. Hindi, Beatles, ABBA, Swahili—all of it.

They circled each other and danced. The music swept Sabine into her dream world, and she tried to perform the movements of the *Bharata Natyam* classical dance taught by Guruji, her dance instructor. The dance was based on emotions expressed in the eyes, face, and body. Gliding like a swan, Sabine raised her arms, fingers curling, closing into a bud. Then her fingers opened up slowly like the petals of a lotus flower.

A thought of Butabika stole her focus, and her steps turned slow and uncertain. She tried to align her hands with the lilting steps of her feet, but if she moved her hands, she forgot her eyes; if she moved her hands and eyes, she forgot her feet; and if she did all three, she forgot the emotions.

"Sabine, you're out of sync," said Zena.

Sabine started again. She recalled Guruji saying, "There's a dance for every mood. If the dance form is angry, show your anger. If the dance form is happy, show your happiness. Dance with feeling. You must dance with feeling."

Sabine felt the tabla beats strike her chest wall. Her feet moved rapidly in tandem to her thudding heart and she found herself spinning erratic little circles round and round like the stray goat. She clapped her hands as the rifle shot went off in her head—*Bang!* Clutching her chest as if in pain, she lowered herself slowly until she lay as still as the dead goat on the cold cement floor.

Zena stopped dancing. She stared down at Sabine. "Our dance is a happy dance, to celebrate Independence Day."

Sabine scrambled to her feet. "I'm sorry." She had danced the goat's fear.

"Beautiful gestures!" It was Ssekore. His gaze locked with Sabine's.

Under the thick lashes, his dark, espresso-hued eyes bore the alertness of the swift impala, after which Kampala had been named. Sabine looked at the way his white fishnet vest outlined his dark neck. His cap was black, yellow, and red, the colours of the Ugandan flag. She felt her face grow hot as the moment stretched out.

"Ssekore, what do you want?" asked Zena in an irritated voice.

He shrugged his broad shoulders. "My dictionary," he said, quickly turning to the plastic shelf against the wall filled with books.

Zena changed the cassette to play African hits, and the girls danced, shaking their shoulders to one beat, hips to another, and knees to another. Often Sabine stole a glance at Ssekore, and smiled at him.

It was noon. Sabine had to leave. Uncle would be waiting outside for her. She and Zena decided to trade back their dresses next time. She put her tape deck into her satchel and said goodbye.

At the front door she ran into Captain Asafa.

"I'm sorry!" he said.

Sabine looked up at his uniform. Her eyes froze on the emblem of a gazelle on his sleeve. Her stomach roiled. Wasn't that the insignia Butabika had?

"Sadru's girl, isn't it? How are you?"

Sabine looked up. His piercing military eyes might fire at her. "I didn't see you. I ..." She couldn't think of anything to say. "I ... I have to go."

She ran across the cement compound and ducked under the clothesline, then climbed into her uncle's waiting car, her legs trembling like the papaya leaves in the wind.

— Home —

In the car, Uncle winked at Sabine in Zena's gomesi. "Met the fairy godmother?"

Sabine, usually quick-witted, paused before nodding. "Too bad the clock struck twelve," she said finally.

Uncle laughed and took off. "I'll take a shorter, faster route home," he said.

Sabine nodded. Hugging her satchel close to her chest, she watched the road through her window, looking out for any military jeeps.

They left Old Kampala behind and drove past the sky-scrapers and big hotels downtown. Beyond the rolling hills of Mengo, the tin shanties of the slums shone like gold in the noon sun. Soon they came upon the familiar sight of tall jac-aranda trees with purple blossoms climbing Nakasero Hill.

Sabine rolled down her window. Red-roofed villas rose like forts penned by neatly trimmed hedges. Where the hedges ended, the iron gates began. Papa told her that during colonial times, only *mzungus*, the whites, and their guard dogs lived in this estate area. After Uganda's independence, the mzungus left, and affluent Indians, including her family, moved in. Sabine was five then. That was also the year Katana began to work for them.

Uncle drove past the servant quarters, Katana's home, hidden behind the overgrown maize stalks. Sabine's family, like other Indian households, followed the mzungus' footsteps in employing an African servant and making sure he lived in close proximity, available at a moment's notice. Katana was away now, visiting his family at his village near Jinja.

Uncle drew up in front of Sabine's house. Tall frangipani trees with white flowers stood upright like sentinels on either side of the porch. Behind the house, rows of leafy green mango trees edged the backyard. Beyond them was a two-metre-high wall topped by barbed wire and shards of glass to keep out *kondos*, machete-armed bandits.

Uncle hugged Sabine. "Remember our pact," he reminded her.

She nodded and got out of the car, then ran up the stone stairway. The brass plate on the intricately carved wooden door from Lamu read SADRU MAHAL. The Palace of Sadru.

The door opened, and Mama stood in a pink salwaar kameez with a matching dupatta drawn over her slim shoulders. Sabine wore the Indian outfit only when she went to mosque. Mama stepped out to talk to Uncle in the car, and Sabine went inside.

Their house was not really a palace, of course, but with its vast open foyer and marble floor it looked too big and too white after Zena's. Sabine's little brother, wearing one of her old dresses, ran to her and she kissed him. His name was Minaz, but she called him Munchkin. Born with

Down syndrome, he hadn't learned to say many words, but he responded to some. He would be nine this year.

"Hey! Big boys don't wear dresses," said Sabine.

Munchkin gurgled, scuffing his feet to make squeaky sounds. Around his neck hung the furry arms of his toy monkey, who had on a yellow jacket and hat, much like Curious George in the books Papa brought home. Sabine called the monkey Milo, after Munchkin's favourite hot chocolate drink. Wherever Munchkin went, Milo went as well.

Mama closed the door behind her. The afternoon light lit up her fair Kashmiri complexion, which shone in stark contrast to her henna-dyed hair, coiffed into an onion-shaped bun.

She pulled Sabine into a warm embrace. "I'm glad you are back. What's this you are wearing?"

"Zena's gown," said Sabine, looking at her mother's pinched face. Mama had more creases in her face than in her dress.

"My eye's been twitching all day. I was scared." Mama caught Sabine's arm.

The touch was soft but charged with electrons of fear. Sabine pulled away. She averted her gaze to the model of the Taj Mahal displayed in the glass cabinet, afraid that Mama would sense something was wrong. She would keep her pact with Uncle.

"Dear, why can't you play with Narmin or Nasrin? They live right here."

"Because ..." Sabine's hands clenched at the names of

her classmates. They were prissy prunes. She'd had a big fight with them after they had said Zena was just *goli*, a "black." Mixing her African and Indian friends was like mixing oil with water.

"Because," said Sabine again. She took off her satchel and flung it onto the sofa, then turned back to look at her mother. Her gaze slid down to her mother's hands, her thumbnail flicking every nail with a click. The clicks grated against Sabine's nerves. She understood her mother's fears but felt irritated by her flicking dance.

Mama tucked a few stray hairs behind her pearl-studded ears. "Your Sunday outings must stop! The streets are filled with soldiers, who have no eyes when they carry guns."

"I know, Mama. I'm not scared," said Sabine, wishing it were true. She stomped across the sitting room, past the kitchen, and out the back door to the yard.

Sabine kicked at the stones and fallen mangoes in her way. She flung off her sandals and climbed the mango tree to her secret cavern made by the overhanging fronds. She called it Paradise Place. Often she hid here when she was in a sour mood. Only Papa knew of her secret spot—once he'd seen her feet peeking out from under the leaves.

Straws of light filtered through the lattice of leaves. She plucked a ripe mango, wiped it with her blouse, and began to eat, the tangy juice dripping down her chin. She decided to call her grandfather at the farm. Whenever her world tipped over, Bapa's breezy tone always set it right. She flung the golden seed as far as she could, slipped down the tree, put on her sandals, and ran inside.

"I miss you, Bapa," Sabine said on the phone.

"And I miss my helper," said Bapa, and he laughed the way he always did. "Cheetah made a catch today."

"Really?" Sabine smiled at the thought. Cheetah was Bapa's golden retriever, who flinched even at flies. The most you got out of him was a bored yawn and a thump-thump of his puny tail. She had named him Cheetah as a joke, hoping one day he would live up to his name as he grew.

"Cheetah bared his teeth, looking as fierce as the real cheetah. He snarled and barked like he'd caught a thief," said Bapa, and paused. "It was a skunk!"

She giggled. "Bapa, things stink here, too. The soldiers act like they own the town."

Bapa wasn't surprised. He said the Africans had been treated as inferior for a long time and so some soldiers liked to show off.

"Yes," she said, thinking of Butabika. "Bapa, it's scary."

"Beta, we're caught in a storm," he said. "Such times can bring out the best or the worst in us. We'll stand like that coffee tree in Kasenda, already so tall and still growing. We'll be challengers like chilies, climbers and sun-seekers like vines."

"Yes, Bapa," she said dutifully. Bapa's examples from his life on the farm did not console her much as she replaced the receiver.

That night, a brown goat stole into Sabine's room in the silence of the dark.

Two pitiful, moist eyes pleaded for help. "Beeeh-ee-eh! Beeeh-ee-eh!"

Sabine touched the soft brown fur, and the goat's face blurred into hers. Then a rifle prodded her chin.

"Indian Princess, say your last words," said the scar-faced soldier.

"Please, I don't want to die," she begged, but the soldier laughed and fired.

Bang! The blood splattered everywhere.

Sabine woke up with a jolt, her bedsheet twisted into a damp rope in her hands. She was alive! But the sight of blood in a dream was a bad omen.

—— The Feather ——

Sabine woke up to the *croo-croo* crowing of a rooster. For a moment she thought she was at Bapa's Kasenda farm. She rubbed her tired eyes, trying to get rid of the sleep. Sunbeams through the eyelets of the lace curtains made gold-beaded patterns on the bed.

She yawned out loud, stretching her legs and arms. Last year, Papa had helped turn her room into a garden. The ceiling was blue and white like the sky, and the rose periwinkles on the rug matched the bedspread. The wall across from the bed was lined with shelves that overflowed with books and beloved objects—skipping stones from the farm, cowrie shells from Bamburi Beach, and her collection of wild animal cards from Brooke Bond tea packets. The side walls were covered with life-size posters of Indian movie stars, and on her bureau near the row of Russian nesting dolls was a photograph of her and Zena in front of the coffee bush that they had planted at Kasenda farm many years ago.

Sabine's blanket fell off her shoulders onto the bed in a heap as she sat up. She heard the crowing again and smiled. It sounded like Katana. She had missed him, his stories, and his songs. He kept their house in tiptop shape;

he dusted the furniture, washed the pots and pans, and washed and ironed their clothes, crediting his thoroughness to his former boss, a mzungu. Katana was proud of the fact that he had worked for a white man. When Katana began to work for her family, he saw Sabine go to school every day and said, "I go, too." So Papa paid his fees for evening classes. Now he was in grade five.

She ran downstairs, across the sitting room to the foyer, and flung open the door. It *was* Katana!

He stood transfixed in the doorway, his gunnysack slung across his shoulder. Papa's old shirt hung on him like an oversized nightshirt. Spiral curls poked out from his torn straw hat like coiled springs of a worn-out sofa. He had only one eye. He had lost the other to an infection when he was a small boy.

"Katana, did the rooster trade jobs with you?"

He didn't reply. His dark face gleamed with streaks of fluorescent white slime, supposedly an ethereal substance. He must have visited the healer at his village and communicated with the spirits of the dead.

"Casper." She teased him fondly. "You look like a ghost."

Katana rocked on his heels and started crowing again.

She giggled. They had expected him to return last Friday, so he was acting silly to cover up his being late. He'd blame the delay on the latest addition or subtraction to his family—"Sorry, my brother died," or "My sister got baby." Sometimes it seemed as if everyone in his village was related to him.

Mama joined them, frowning. "Your porridge will get cold," she told Sabine. Then she turned to Katana. "I don't want to hear stories of why you're late. The house is dusty. Bwana's shirts and Sabine's uniforms need ironing. *Chup, chup!*" She snapped her fingers.

"Yes, Mama Guli," he said, and padded after Mama into the kitchen in his lime-green flip-flops. Sabine followed them. Katana and Mama often quibbled. At every opportunity he'd sneak outside into the backyard to read, which drove Mama into a frenzy.

"Sabine, I bring *zawadi*, gift for you," said Katana. He slipped the sack off his shoulder, dug inside, and brought out a bunch of matoke.

"Thank you," said Sabine. He always brought green plantain for her.

He walked to the sink and sang in English. He tried to speak as much English as he could because he was eager to master the white man's language.

Sabine ate her porridge. She could hear Katana sing as he washed the dishes. *O feather, tickle the hippo, poke the rhino, but kill the hyena. O feather, sweep b-i-i-g troubles far, far, far.*

Munchkin screamed, awakening, and Mama hurried upstairs to him.

"Do you want some chai?" Sabine asked Katana.

He smiled his schoolboy smile, wiped his hands, and reached up to the top shelf for his plastic mug. Sabine poured the tea for him, and he dumped in five spoonfuls of sugar. He loved sweet tea. Last month Mama noticed that the sugar level in the jar had dipped and warned him,

"Worms will grow in your stomach." But he just laughed it off.

Sabine diddled with her spoon in her bowl of porridge. "How big is little Sabine now?" she asked. That was his daughter, named after her.

Grinning eagerly, he raised his arms to indicate his daughter's height. He drank the last dregs of tea, turned back to make sure Mama was not around, and said, "Sabine, I tell you something important."

"Okay," she said.

He always told her stories. Stories of Kintu, the first man on earth, and of Shamu the serpent, who swallowed its tail. And if she didn't finish her meal he'd sing, *The wicked witch of Wala-Wala, Shoko-loko-bango-sheh is riding a hyena, grabbing girls who don't eat. Crunch, munch, you want to be her lunch?*

The pupil of his eye dilated. "Spirits under *mbuyu* warn me ..."

Sabine recoiled. Of all his stories, the myth of the baobab tree chilled her to the marrow. Her mind replayed the baobab song he used to sing to her long ago. *The bad-luck mbuyu, oh the mbuyu, it grew up, up, up, and its roots grew down, down, down.* She remembered too well how after playing under the baobab in their backyard one day, she'd caught a high fever and was delirious. Dr. Shah said she had malaria and prescribed bitter quinine, but Katana insisted the spirits had possessed her. Papa ordered the baobab cut down, and she recovered.

"No baobab stories, please."

He drew closer as if to share a secret. "The spirits under the mbuyu warn me. The Countdown Monster eat you."

"What about you?"

"I be safe." He pointed to the white slime on his face. "I be scared for you."

"There are no monsters," she said firmly. She rose and carried her bowl of unfinished porridge to the sink.

He followed her with his mug. "I, seventh son of my mother, know."

"Why me?"

He looked down at her feet. "'Cause you got new shoes." He looked up. "'Cause you be pretty." He licked his lips. "'Cause Dada Amin no like you."

"Katana, I'm Ugandan like you."

"I get a magic to save you." He took his sack from the cabinet under the sink and dug out a chicken feather, white as snow.

"Thank you," she said, accepting it.

Katana's magic was strange but genuine. One day last April, Papa woke up to find the left side of his face paralyzed. When he spoke, his speech was slurred. When he smiled, only one side of his face moved. Mama arranged for special prayers to be recited for him at the mosque for seven days. Right on the seventh day, Papa felt a faint movement in his cheek and Mama exclaimed triumphantly, "Such is the power of God." But unbeknownst to Mama, Papa had been rubbing the blood of a dead parrot on his cheek from Katana's healer. Papa recovered fully.

Sabine held the feather away. It smelled awful, but she didn't say anything. She slipped it in her pocket.

"If anybody shoot you, *dishoom!*" He pointed two fingers at her like a gun. "The bullet become water," he said.

She nodded. She didn't want to argue with him. She had learned about the Maji Maji Rebellion of 1905 in Tanganyika, in which the Africans were told by a witch doctor that if they sprinkled a special *maji,* water, on their chests, they would be protected from bullets fired by the German colonials. The bullets were said to miraculously turn into water. But the rebellion had left several hundred Germans and seventy-five thousand Africans dead.

She ran upstairs to get ready for school. Standing in front of her dresser in her well-pressed uniform, she brushed her wild hair that spiked and snarled every which way. Scads of one-eleven scars swam over her reflection. Quickly she pulled the feather from her pocket. The scars vanished.

If only Katana had given her the talisman earlier, she would have used it on the mad Butabika.

O feather, sweep b-i-i-g troubles far, far, far. She sang Katana's song as she twirled across the room, her eyes on the feather in her spiraling hands, the spirals rising higher and higher. Then she jumped, the arc of a diving dolphin, and landed gracefully, pleased by her smooth, flowing gestures. Now she knew: when she danced, her head and her heart must go together. Where the hand goes, the eyes follow; where the eyes are, the mind follows.

"Everything will be fine," she said loudly.

— Lalita —

"Today is day twelve. Seventy-eight days remain for foreign Indians to leave Uganda."

The countdown on the radio was drowned out by the clanging doorbell. Sabine closed her mystery novel and ran to the door, with Mama following closely after her. Uncle was coming for supper today, and Mama had cooked masala kingfish, his favourite meal.

It was Lalita. Gold-embroidered butterflies decorated her fire-red sari, the pleats folded perfectly and tucked into her tiny waist. She must own a sari of every colour. Her hair, tied in a bun, was held by strings of jasmine. A bird's nest. What did the queen want?

Sabine and Zena called Lalita the queen because she carried herself regally. The girls often ate at Lalita's teahouse, and sometimes when they paid the bill the queen did not return their change. "Remind me next time, okay?" she'd say. Zena cornered the queen once, but she said, "Oh, silly me," slapping her forehead to indicate a loss of memory, and walked off without bringing the change.

Lalita folded her hands in greeting. The red dot on her forehead shone like a third eye. Swinging her hips, she danced across the foyer in her *latak-matak* style, her hula-hoop earrings swinging and the gold bangles on her fair arms tinkling.

"How are you, Guli-*bhen*?" She called Mama sister, and so became Sabine's aunt.

Lalita beckoned to Sabine and kissed her noisily. Oh! The strong scent of lavender pressed from a million flowers tickled Sabine's nostrils and gave her a sneezing fit as she followed her mother and Lalita to the sitting room.

Sabine sat on the far side of the room, pretending to read but watching Lalita from the corner of her eye. Lalita settled herself daintily on the damask sofa, crossed her legs, and adjusted the fold of her sari. Red toenails peeped out from sandals with gold straps.

"Where's my sweet-sweet Mithoo?" Lalita's voice shrilled across the room. Sabine gnashed her teeth.

Munchkin bounded from the kitchen with his Milo, squealing as he climbed onto Lalita's lap. She lowered her head to nuzzle him. "My Mithoo, sweeter than sugar, na?"

Munchkin cooed, pulling her diamond nose ring, exploring every part of her face.

Katana knocked on the door and came in carrying a tray with glasses of Vimto. Lalita accepted a glass politely and waited for him to leave before she spoke again. Munchkin began to fidget in her lap, and she held the glass while he slurped through the straw, gurgling.

"Your brother's coming today for supper, na?" Lalita asked.

Mama nodded.

Lalita leaned closer to Mama and whispered, "I need

Zully Passport to get me a work permit so I can keep my teahouse open until I get my visa from the British."

Uncle was known as Zully Passport in the Indian community because his influence with immigration officials enabled him to get passports and permits with a minimum of hassle. Since the passage of the expulsion law, he'd been flooded with immigration requests.

Lalita snapped open her gold purse. Munchkin pulled at it. "No-no," she said, pulling out a brown envelope, her talon-like nails as red as her sensuous lips. She held out the envelope to Mama. "Please give this to Zully."

Frowning, Mama accepted the envelope. She placed it under the crystal bowl of pomegranates on the ebony table in the centre of the room.

"I hope the silly British give the visas fast-fast. Every Indian and his dog is leaving town. What about you?"

Mama shrugged. "We are Ugandan citizens."

"Citizen, bitizen, does it matter?" Lalita giggled. "You are Indians, na?"

"Aunty, we are not quitters!" The words spilled from Sabine before she knew. She saw her mother's killing look and quickly apologized. "I'm sorry," she said, though she didn't quite feel sorry.

"*Ar're*, those who go to the river early get to drink clean water." Pleased with her comeback, Lalita flashed her winner's smile. She turned back to Mama. "Guli-bhen, we can't trust the blacks, they're all *char-so-vis*."

Sabine seethed. Char-so-vis, the number 420 in Gujarati dialect, signified crooks.

"The crooks will bother us even if we're already in the ground."

Sabine was about to remind the queen that Hindus are cremated, not buried, when Munchkin pulled at Lalita's gold earring. Good job, Sabine cheered him silently.

"No-no-no." Lalita bounced Munchkin on her lap. She turned to Mama. "They call us Jews. I tell you, we're far too successful for our safety. Look." She placed her arm next to Mama's. "I'm Hindu, you are Muslim. But we're the same colour, na?"

Mama nodded, cracking the joints in her hand. *Crack. Crack. Crack.*

"Haven't you seen soldiers in jeeps painting the town red?"

Sabine tensed.

"Go, Guli-bhen, go. I'm telling you for your own good." Lalita often dispensed unasked-for advice. "We must be two steps ahead of the blacks. Go before it's too late."

Go, the voice screamed in Sabine's ears. The page of her novel crumpled. *Go*, said the countdown on the radio every hour. Her damp palms were smudged with ink, the page a sodden wad. The *go, go, go* beats struck her head.

She summoned the calmest tone she could manage. "Aunty," she said politely, "what if you don't get your visa in time? Where will you go?"

"No worries, dear. Aunty has one leg here, one leg there. I have a British passport, Uncle Viram has the Indian." She smirked. "We are—what's the saying? Ah, 'Looking

London, Talking Tokyo,' but we are talking Bombay." She giggled. "Let the whites bark about their quota. In the end they will have to take us; they have no choice. But those who stay here, oh-ho!" She rubbed her manicured hands like a conspirator. "They'll boil and bubble in this pressure cooker."

Sabine was livid. What did the queen think she was? A fortune-teller? She was scaring Mama. The queen was jealous that she had been expelled while they could stay.

Sabine tried to catch Munchkin's eye. When he looked her way, she raised her fist, making sure he saw it, then surreptitiously put it behind her as if she was hiding something. It was mean of her, but she had to do it to rescue her mother.

Munchkin hopped off Lalita's lap and ran to Sabine. He put Milo down and tried to pry open her fingers. Making sure no one was looking, she grabbed Milo with her other hand and hid the monkey under the pillow behind her.

"Eeeeee!" Munchkin screamed, pulling Sabine's hair.

The distraction worked. Mama leapt to her feet and took Munchkin, still crying, in her arms. "I'm sorry," she said. "Minaz is tired. You'll have to excuse me."

Lalita rose at once. Her hand slipped inside her sari blouse and brought out her house keys. She pulled her sari flap across her chest and over her head, then raised her folded hands to the ceiling to address her god. "Ram, Ram," she said, and left.

Sabine smiled.

── The Fight ──

August 17, 1972
DAY 12

That evening the house was full of the spicy aroma of sizzling kingfish by the time Papa came home from work. He had returned from his business trip the day before.

Sabine met Papa in the foyer, and Munchkin ran after her. Papa's dark suit matched his raven-black hair, coaxed into place by styling cream. He held Sabine, smoothing her tangles away from her eyes, as she inhaled his musky aftershave lotion. Munchkin prodded and pushed Sabine, wanting to be included in the embrace. Papa lifted him and they rubbed their noses together, to Munchkin's delight.

They joined Mama on the sofa in the sitting room.

Papa hugged Mama. "Guli, I'm starving. I could eat an elephant."

Mama smiled and said that Zully would join them for supper. Katana set the table and left. Sabine called Uncle Zully at his home, but there was no answer.

Papa tweaked his mustache. "When will your brother learn to keep time?"

Mama frowned. "He must be delayed by some urgent work."

"You mean his drink at Karibu Bar," said Papa.

Sabine sensed a fight brewing between her parents. "Let's eat," she said. "Uncle can join us later."

They ate in silence. The only noise was that of forks clinking against plates. Uncle's delay had created tension that was as hot and spicy as the kingfish they ate. Mama cut the fish into pieces and removed the bones from Munchkin's portion.

"Mmm ... delicious," said Sabine to dissipate the tension.

"The fish is from Malalo, the farmer you saw last week," said Mama.

Papa nodded. His clients often brought gifts in appreciation of his help.

"I hope Zully's okay," said Mama. "These are bad times."

"A rain cloud," said Papa, thrusting his fork into the fish, "will clear up."

"I don't think so." Mama's eyes darkened.

"Papa's right," said Sabine, and she caught a hint of a smile in his face.

"Finish your fish." Mama pointed to Sabine's plate.

"I'm eating," Sabine said, frowning. It was Mama who wasn't eating.

Munchkin pointed to the ketchup. Sabine squeezed the bottle for him. Red sauce plopped out like lumps of congealed blood. Suddenly she wasn't hungry.

"Sadru, Lalita says everybody's leaving."

"Everybody who's British," said Papa, swallowing a forkful of food. "But we are—body, soul, and by law—one hundred percent Ugandan."

Sabine's jaw clenched. The queen had planted a bomb of fear in Mama's head.

"Lalita says the President's like Hitler," said Mama.

Papa shook with laughter. "*Njingo! Kichwa maji.* The fool's head is filled with water." He clicked his tongue, making splashy sounds like a shaking coconut. Munchkin copied Papa. Ordinarily Sabine would have giggled, but now she smiled weakly, her mind jumbled with the contradictory views of the President. Hitler? Fool? Hero?

The countdown came again on the radio. "Today is day twelve. Seventy-eight days remain for foreign Indians to leave Uganda."

Sabine shifted uneasily.

Mama put down her fork. "Sadru, we should leave even if we're citizens."

"And go where? Tanzania?" Papa's mocking voice cut as sharp as the knife in his hand. "You want to give up our farms and factories to Nyerere?" President Nyerere, friend of deposed Ugandan President Obote, had confiscated people's shops, businesses, and houses in Tanzania in support of socialism.

"We can go to your sister Parin in Kenya, maybe," said Mama.

"Kenya says it will soon copy Amin, kick out Indians who aren't Kenyans."

"But we can stay for a few weeks," said Mama. "Come back after the countdown."

"And who'll look after my businesses?" asked Papa.

Mama shrugged her slim shoulders.

"And don't tell me you want to go to India, because it, too, has slammed its door, saying they can't feed their own."

"Lalita's lucky—she can go to England."

Papa stared at Mama. "The British quota will accept only three thousand Indians each year! They have stabbed the backs of forty thousand British Indians, saying that England is a crowded little island. You know how long it will take before all of them can go?"

"Over thirteen years," blurted Sabine, satisfied at being able to make the calculation quickly. "I'm so glad we are Ugandan citizens. We can stay here."

Papa nodded. "Scared roosters can fly, but we'll stay here. This is our home!"

Mama looked down at her plate filled with fish and said nothing.

Sabine tried to reassure her mother. "Papa, they can't expel so many people so fast, can they? Surely the Americans will intervene."

Papa smiled cynically. "The Yankee Doodles don't care, dear. Didn't you learn in history class about our dark continent? Africa is not of strategic importance to them."

"Then we are trapped." Mama's shrill voice broke. "The soldiers will kill us!"

Clang! Sabine's fork hit the floor as she recalled her encounter with Butabika.

"Gulshan," Papa said firmly. That was Mama's full name. The black hairs on his mustache bristled. "You are frightening Sabine."

"I'm fine," said Sabine, picking up the fork. She wanted to kick herself for being clumsy. Her heart and mind fought a war. She understood Mama's fears and yearned to comfort her, but she believed Papa knew best. Suddenly, the fish in her mouth tasted bad.

"What about Sabine?" Mama asked. "You know girls are more vulnerable."

"Sabine's my brave boy." Papa smiled at her.

Sabine returned the smile, even though she knew she was neither brave nor his son. Sons were the pride of Indian families; a son inherited the family wealth and preserved the family name, unlike a daughter, who married and took on her husband's family name. But after Munchkin was born with Down syndrome, Papa had vested all his hopes in her as the sole keeper of their family legacy.

Mama looked at Papa accusingly. "Don't put ideas in Sabine's head. She's a girl. She'll always be a girl. I think we should send her to boarding school in England."

Didn't Mama love her? "I'm not going to a stinking boarding school in some dumb place." How could she leave her family, Uncle, Bapa and Kasenda farm, Zena and Ssekore?

Papa pushed his plate away and rose. His face was red and his temple pulsed. Sabine could imagine the blood coursing through it. "Guli, we are fine here. The sky hasn't fallen and the earth's still moving on its axis." As his fist slammed down and struck the table to deliver his final verdict, both Sabine in her seat and the cutlery on the table jumped. "We will stay here."

—

Later, when Mama took Munchkin up to bed, Papa put his arm around Sabine and led her through the French doors to his office. She had been there once before. It also had its own separate entrance from outside that was used by visitors when they came to see Papa for business.

Papa closed the doors behind her. Sabine felt important and special.

A rosewood desk engraved with a lattice of lotus flowers sat in the middle of the office, and along the walls the shelves were filled with thick old books in leather bindings. Red encyclopedias with gold lettering were arranged in alphabetical order.

Papa led her to the black sculpture by the desk; it was as tall as she was. "Do you know what this artifact represents?"

She shook her head. "But I know who made it. The Makonde tribesmen."

"Yes." Papa smiled. "It is the Tree of Life."

She touched the sculpture and felt its rocklike hardness.

"It depicts past and present generations supporting each other."

She nodded, awed. When she first saw the sculpture, it looked like a bunch of acrobats holding on to each other in weird positions.

"Bapa and I are down here and you are standing on our shoulders." Papa took her hand and placed it on top of the sculpture and looked into her eyes. "You are the child of pioneers, a pedigree breed."

Sabine's face burned with pride, the heat of a thousand suns.

"Our roots run deep. Bapa came here with bare hands, bare feet, empty pockets, but he accomplished what a hundred men couldn't."

"I know, Papa."

Bapa had told her about his voyage from India, how he crossed the Indian Ocean in a small dhow. The British colonials indentured him and other Indians to build the Kenya-Uganda railway. Bapa had laid tracks in the jungle for months. Some of his friends died of malaria; others were dragged from their camps to their death by man-eating lions.

"Sabine, you are Simba's grandchild. This land is your oyster. One day Bapa's farms and my business will be yours. I have big dreams for you. Don't worry, things will get better."

"Yes, Papa," said Sabine, her every nerve end on fire.

Papa believed in her, but did she believe in herself?

That night Sabine called Uncle several times, but there was no answer. She hoped he had not met with an accident. He did drive fast sometimes.

—— Where Is Uncle? ——

August 18, 1972
DAY 13

Sabine's head reeled from the disgraceful incident at school that day. Army officials had grabbed the British school principal, Mr. Corky, removed his shoes to humiliate him, and dragged him away in his socks into a waiting military jeep outside. What wrong could old Corky have done?

Many of Sabine's other teachers and classmates were leaving the country. And Guruji, her dance instructor, had called to say that she was leaving. *Everybody is running away.*

Sabine sank into the soft pile of the sitting room carpet with the model car kit Papa had brought from his trip. It had the parts for assembling three vehicles: a lorry like Bapa's Bedford, a double-decker bus, and a sports coupe like Uncle's. Cars were Uncle's passion. Mama said the first word he spoke as a child was *car*. Sabine smiled. She'd assemble the sports car model for Uncle and give it to him for his birthday next month. She'd tease him. *I bought you a car!*

Excited, she placed the hood, wheels, and axle on the coffee table and read the instructions. Katana's melodic voice drifted from the kitchen—*O feather, help Sabine, Simba's grandchild.* The lyrics were punctuated by the thwapping sounds of his yellow dust rag slapping the furniture. Old Corky was the one who needed help, she thought, not her.

Munchkin burst into the room with Milo. He knelt near her, and she felt his warm breath on her neck. He grabbed some parts of the car, uttering joyous sounds.

"No! Play with Milo."

She wrestled to get the parts back, but gave up when she saw Mama stagger into the room, her hands covering her face, sobbing.

"What's wrong, Mama?" Sabine asked, helping her mother to the sofa. She sat down, too, and put her hand on her mother's arm.

Mama sniffed. "Zully's gone."

Goose bumps dotted Sabine's arm. "What do you mean, gone?"

"Zully's not home, not at his shop, not in any bars."

"And his car?"

"Missing as well."

"Mama, Uncle must have gone on his adventure trip." Mama always overreacted, thought Sabine. Uncle had the gypsy spirit in him. Often he took off in his car and called later to say where he was. She handed a box of tissues to her mother and draped her pashmina shawl over her trembling shoulders.

Mama's unsteady voice came through the tissue. "He didn't come for supper."

Sabine nodded. That was a bit strange. "I'm sure he'll call in a day or two."

"Mama Guli." Katana offered her a glass of water. He carried Munchkin, who seemed near tears as well, and sat on the floor with him. He tickled Munchkin to make him laugh. "Minazi be good boy," he said. He picked up the magazine on the ebony table and showed him the pictures.

Sabine held Mama's cold hand and reminded her that last year when Uncle had taken off, he called them a few days later from Bamburi Beach in Mombasa.

Uncle often felt compelled to drive hundreds of kilometres as if searching for a missing part of himself that would make his life meaningful. Mama repeatedly told him to get married, but he laughed it off, saying, "I can't look after both *ladi* and *gadi*." Brides and cars both needed maintenance. He'd chosen cars.

Papa came home from work and reassured Mama. "Don't worry. Zully's smitten with the travel bug." He picked up the fallen end of Mama's shawl, wound it round her shoulder, and drew her closer.

"I have a bad feeling," mumbled Mama, pale as the ivory bangle on her arm. Her fingers unlaced and then knit again.

Mama's bad feeling gnawed at Sabine as well. Was Uncle okay? What if …

"Ha! You know Zully. He can appear and disappear like a genie," Papa replied.

Mama nodded, but reluctantly, it seemed to Sabine.

At night, Sabine's bedside radio spat out the countdown, that same stern voice. "Today is day thirteen. Seventy-seven days remain for foreign Indians to leave Uganda."

Thirteen. She repeated the unlucky number aloud. But didn't the Egyptians regard it as lucky? What of African mythology? She would have to ask Katana. She stared at the ceiling for a long time without coming to a definitive answer.

She tried to sleep, but could not. She rose and strapped her anklet on. *Uncle, this dance is for you.* She danced with frenzied energy, shaking her head like a whirling dervish, right arm pointing to the stars in the heavens and left arm to the floor. She danced until sweat poured down her face. She danced until her arms and legs no longer felt like hers.

Still, she couldn't sleep. She took out her car kit from the drawer of her night table and began to assemble the model car for Uncle. Things would fall into place by Uncle's birthday.

— Little India —

August 20–26, 1972
DAYS 15–21

On Sunday, Papa dropped Sabine off in Little India. Today she and Zena planned to buy the fabric for their dance costumes. Sabine's seamstress would sew her outfit, and Zena would stitch her own.

Sabine saw Zena as she hopped off the public bus. How beautiful she looked in her kanga pantsuit. As she drew near, Sabine read the Swahili text on the border of Zena's blouse. Translated into English, it said, Patience can cook a stone. Every kanga cloth featured a central motif with a new saying. When the kiosk owners got supplies of kanga with new sayings, Zena had told her, there was always a mad rush to buy them.

The girls greeted each other and skipped along the narrow winding alleys where spices twanged noses and Hindi songs blared. Women in bright saris tugged small children, chatting loudly in Hindi. Indian tailors sat on stools along the length of the pavement, foot-pedalling Singer sewing machines.

Sabine told Zena about Uncle. "I hope he calls soon," said Sabine.

They rounded the corner and bumped into Amina Goli.

Amina stood before them, larger than life, in her usual low-waisted checked dress and a white skullcap. Everybody knew Amina Goli. The police chased away other beggars but turned a blind eye to her.

Tink-tink. Amina rattled her can, then turned sideways to draw attention to her bruised cheek smeared with iodine, her newfound malady.

The girls giggled. Amina sported a new affliction every week. She never talked. Some people said she faked being mute to boost her collection.

"*Pole*, sorry," said Zena, dropping a five-cent coin into Amina's tomato soup can.

Amina nodded, then thrust the can at Sabine, who also took out a five-cent coin. But Amina rattled the can loudly to protest the diddly amount.

"Okay," said Sabine, and came up with a ten-cent coin.

But Amina pulled back the can with a throaty screech.

Zena giggled. "She knows you are *Wa-benzi*."

Sabine smiled. Owners of Mercedes-Benz cars were referred to as Wa-benzi. Amina must have seen her in Papa's car when he dropped her off.

The crafty Amina extracted her toll based on which of the three *W* classes in Uganda the giver belonged to. Wazungus, the whites, at the top of the pack, had to give her currency bills; wahindi, the Indians, silver coins; and wananchi, the ethnic Africans, could get away with copper coins. Age, too, was a factor. If Mama were here, Amina would settle for nothing less than five silver shillings.

Sabine dug into her coin purse and found a *sumni*, a fifty-cent silver coin, which Amina accepted gleefully. She bent and plucked a bougainvillea floret from the hedge that lined the road and handed it to Sabine with a flourish and a smile.

"Thank you," said Sabine, and she clipped the pink floret in her hair.

Sabine and Zena window-shopped for sari fabrics all day. Some stores had closed down, as the owners were British Indians. Other stores hung big cloth banners: Closing Sale. Buy one, get two free.

Bombay Silks displayed fabrics in new colours in their window—frosty pink, shimmering saffron, midnight blue, turquoise ice—and Zena got all excited. Pointing to a bolt of silver fabric, she said breathlessly, "Let's check it out."

Inside, the store brimmed with smoky sandalwood incense. Wooden shelves were stacked with bolts of brightly coloured silk, satin, and chiffon from India. Hindi hits blared from a tiny transistor radio. The red-turbaned owner, Mr. Singh, came running to serve them. His blacker-than-black beard covered most of his face.

"What you want?" he asked in thick, Hindi-accented English.

"Can you show us that fabric, please?" Zena pointed at the window.

"Ha, yes!" said Mr. Singh, smiling at Sabine as if she were a shiny shilling from the mint.

Sabine shrugged. It was Zena, not she, who had asked.

Mr. Singh brought out the bolt of silver fabric and unrolled some of it on the counter. "This is miracle cloth, jersey nylon, shipped all the way from India." He creased some of the diaphanous fabric in his hand and released it. "Permanent press. No need to iron." He looked at Sabine. "Your price."

Zena stroked the fabric to feel the texture, and Mr. Singh pulled back the bolt.

"My friend wants to buy the fabric," said Sabine, alarmed at his rude action.

"*Baprebap!*" he exclaimed, rolling his eyes. "I think she your ayah."

Embarrassment robbed Sabine of a reply, but Zena was quick to respond. "I will buy the fabric later, after your shop's taken over by wananchi."

Mr. Singh's hands flew up in the air as if he had been caught in a holdup, and his jaw opened and closed, a shark washed ashore.

The girls walked out of the store laughing, tears running down their cheeks.

"I'm glad Dada Amin is weeding out foreign Indians," said Zena.

Sabine nodded. But Mr. Singh had always been polite when she went to his shop with Mama.

Zena and Sabine found a similar fabric in the next store. They bought it, and Sabine was relieved.

Back home, Sabine found that Uncle still hadn't called.

Mama wrung her hands as if squeezing dirty water from

a rag. "Do you think Zully has met with an accident?"

Papa shook his head. "They'd find his car."

"Do you think he's in trouble over his ... umm, passport business?"

Papa shook his head again, when the phone rang. Sabine leapt to her feet, hoping it was Uncle. *Please please please.*

But it was Bapa, inquiring if they had any news.

Monday evening, Sabine's family sat in the sitting room unusually silent. Currents of uneasiness churned underneath the cover of silence. Munchkin, sitting on Mama's lap, watched television. Papa hid behind the newspaper. They had still not heard from Uncle.

Mama cleared her throat. "Sadru, we should report Zully as missing."

"Mama's right," said Sabine, hoping desperately she was wrong. "Uncle can't be on a holiday for this long and not call us."

Papa folded the *Uganda Argus* and rose. "I'll call good old Commissioner Karanja. He should know." Papa and Commissioner Karanja had attended the same college in England.

After he hung up, Papa told them Mr. Karanja would set up a police inquiry to investigate Uncle's disappearance, but the results could take a few days, as the number of disappearances in Uganda was on the rise.

All week, Sabine could not concentrate in school. At home, the radio spewed the countdown every hour. The stern voice irritated her, but she did not switch it off in case the news mentioned Uncle.

The police inquiry did not yield any results. They referred Papa to the Public Safety Unit, run by army officers. So every day after work Papa waited in a long line at the PSU office to find out if they had any information on Uncle. But each time Papa was dismissed with a one-word reply: *Sijui*, I don't know.

Every day Papa came home late in the evening and collapsed into his armchair, his weary face in stark contrast to his crisp suit. Sabine felt sorry for him.

She tried to be helpful at home. She assembled the lorry and the double-decker bus in the car kit for Munchkin and played car crash with him. She taught him to colour. She answered the phone. Most of the calls were from the workers at Uncle's car shop, wanting to find out if Uncle was back. They had lost their jobs, their income, and their families were hungry.

Bapa phoned every day to ask about Uncle.

"Sabine, Kasuku can talk!"

"Really?" How hard Sabine had tried last time to teach the African Grey parrot at the farm to say her name, but it only stared dumbly at her.

"It swore at Halima today."

Sabine laughed. Halima was the manager of Bapa's farm and also Zena and Ssekore's aunt.

"'Shut up! Shut up!'" Bapa imitated Kasuku's squeaky voice on the phone.

Sabine laughed again.

"Sometimes, Beta, things take longer than you or I wish."

"Yes, Bapa," she said, thinking of the saying on the blouse that Zena had been wearing earlier. *Patience can cook a stone.* Sabine wouldn't have minded the long wait if only she knew that Uncle was safe.

— Lalita's Teahouse —

August 27, 1972

DAY 22

Sabine stepped out of Papa's car in Little India and waved to him as he took off. Today she and Zena had decided to meet at Lalita's teahouse. She ambled along the spice-scented alley, past the tailors on the pavement, their heads bent over sewing machines that chuffed and clanked. Chatty women in saris, their baskets bursting with the day's bargains, brushed past her. The mystery of Uncle's disappearance had dug a dark pit into which Sabine seemed to slip deeper every day. How could he vanish?

She found herself walking toward Uncle's car shop as if pulled by an invisible force. The steel door of Zully Motors was bolted. She lingered in the parking lot filled with rows of used cars for sale, scrutinizing the road, searching for signs of blood or any evidence of a struggle—a torn piece of a shirt or a paper. Nothing.

Slowly she breathed out the tightness that constricted her chest and pulled herself away, forcing one foot before the other to the bus stop where she was meeting Zena.

The Curry Pot teahouse was filled with customer chatter and laughter amid the blare of the latest Hindi songs from the radio. The tables were crowded, mostly with Indians sipping cardamom chai. It looked like Bombay in the Hindi movies, Sabine thought.

"Ahhh!" said Zena, taking in the tantalizing smells. She loved Indian food.

They joined the line of customers to place their orders. Queen Lalita guarded the till in a gold-spangled azure-blue sari, the veil pulled over her head in a show of modesty. Her ears, neck, and arms were covered with gold.

"Comes from the planet of gold," Zena whispered.

"Catch her without clothes, but never without gold," Sabine whispered back, and Zena laughed. Soon it was their turn to order.

"Haaallo, haaallo." Lalita's diamond nose ring flashed a brilliant blue.

People said the queen's nose ring caught unwary customers in her hypnotic spell, making them tip generously. If you escaped this trap, you were ensnared in the next one—charged for additional items you hadn't ordered. Despite this, people poured in like rain. They loved the food.

"Any news of Zully?" Lalita asked, her kohl-lined eyes fluttering.

Sabine shook her head and swallowed a rush of sadness.

"Ah! Without Zully's help, these doors will close," Lalita said in a voice of regret; then she stopped as she eyed Zena. "What will you girls eat?" she asked. Her sari slipped off her head, exposing a bun held by strings of jasmine.

After Sabine had placed the order, someone in the kitchen behind the counter called out for Lalita, and she left.

Zena nudged Sabine. "I thought your uncle ran a car dealership."

"Yes, but he helps people get work permits so they can keep their businesses open."

Zena's blackberry eyes widened. "But that's *magendo*. It's illegal."

"Not really." A sharpness edged Sabine's voice. "I'll explain later," she said as she saw that Lalita was coming back.

But then there was another call for Lalita. She huffed back into the kitchen and yelled at her workers, "You make my blood boil!"

"I'll be at the table," Zena told Sabine, and left.

Lalita stormed back to the counter. "These magicians," she said to Sabine, meaning her workers. "When my back's turned, the butter, sugar, flour, all vanish."

Sabine glanced through the glass door of the kitchen and saw that all the workers were Africans. "But Aunty, how would you run this café without them?"

"I suppose." Lalita tucked a strand of hair behind her ear just as an African waiter arrived with the girls' order, cups of steamy, spicy tea and a platter of samosas and kebabs. He followed Sabine to the table where Zena sat:

"You were telling me about your uncle," said Zena, savouring a crispy samosa.

"Uncle helps those who are treated unfairly by the government."

"Like the queen," Zena said tartly.

Sabine swallowed. "Zena, is it fair if the government

decides your career? Remember Aziz, my second cousin?"
She explained how Aziz had gotten the highest grades on
his exams and had applied to study medicine, but the government assigned him a place in the agriculture school at
Makerere University instead. They wanted only African
doctors.

Zena nodded, chewing quietly.

Sabine dipped a samosa into the tamarind chutney and
popped it in her mouth before continuing. "So poor Aziz
applied to a medical college in Iran and was accepted, but
immigration officials refused to let him go."

Suddenly a hush fell. The busy waiters, scurrying with
trays of food balanced precariously in their hands, froze.
Only the rusty fan in the ceiling buzzed. Three soldiers
had stomped into the teahouse.

Sabine's skin prickled.

Lalita thrust out her chest and stepped forward, the
golden border of her sari lifting in little waves over her
sandaled heels. She appraised the soldiers critically with
those kohl-lined eyes that trusted no one. "What do you
want?" she asked.

Not bothering to reply, the soldiers scanned the room.
One short soldier barked, "Why is there no photograph of
our beloved president?"

Sabine gazed at the bare white walls of the teahouse
around her.

"The place will close down soon anyway," said Lalita.
"What do you want?" she asked again, her tone danger-
ously overbearing.

"You," said the short soldier, grinning.

"Me?" said Lalita dramatically.

"Yes, Mama India. You are under arrest."

"Why? I have done nothing wrong."

The soldier raised his voice. "You tore down Dada Amin's photo."

"I didn't tear down any photo-bhoto." Lalita's hands flew to her hips in defiance.

Sabine cringed. Fire had met fire. The accusation was false, but you couldn't defy military might. She recalled the plight of the taxi driver who dared to honk at the soldier. Lalita's defiance was dangerous; she might not know what they could do, but Sabine knew.

The soldier poked a finger on Lalita's exposed midriff, as fair as Bamburi sand.

"Don't touch me!" Lalita shrank back.

He grinned and poked her again. The other soldiers grabbed Lalita's arms and twisted them behind her back, making her gold bangles tinkle.

"Ram, Ram!" Lalita, now visibly frightened, cried her god's name.

But army law counted more than any Indian god's law, thought Sabine, looking around at the pale faces of customers. Then her hand in her pocket rubbed against the magic feather Katana had given her, and she sprang up.

"Aunty, Viram Uncle gave me the photo. I took it to have it framed."

She felt a kick to her shin under the table and met Zena's stare, but ignored it.

"Aah! That old photo," said the clever Lalita. "It needed a stretch and a nice gold frame." She turned to the soldiers. "I'm sorry," she said in a wounded tone.

The soldiers released her, but the short one approached Sabine's table. "Where did you take it, young lady?" he asked, his eyes pinched like fennel seeds.

Caught in the soldier's piercing glare, Sabine felt as if a blood vessel would burst in her thumping head. "Moonlight Studio," she blurted. It was next to Uncle's car shop.

"How long will it take?"

"It will be ready by ..." Her tongue locked.

"Monday," Lalita interjected, and Sabine nodded. "Yes, Monday," she said.

One brave customer came to their aid. "*Rafiki,* friend," he said to the soldiers, "let's eat in peace."

"Yes, yes," murmured a few others.

The soldiers stomped out of the teahouse as abruptly as they had entered it. The feather had worked! Sabine beamed as the customers cheered.

Zena pushed her bowl away and rose, her chair screeching against the cement floor. Sabine rose to follow Zena but found herself wrapped in Lalita's arms.

"You are brave like your Papa."

"Aunty, I have to go," Sabine said. She rushed out and caught up with Zena a few steps from the teahouse.

"You lied to help the queen," said Zena, not looking at Sabine.

"They lied first," said Sabine.

Zena scowled. "But why did you help her? She's British.

She's not one of us."

"Lalita's my neighbour and Mama's friend."

"Well, I don't like her." Zena quickened her pace.

"Neither do I, but I don't like those soldiers either. Zena, you don't know them."

"I know them very well. I told you before, my uncle's a fine soldier."

Zena walked briskly to the bus stop and climbed into a waiting bus, leaving Sabine standing all by herself.

— The Midnight Train —

Lalita told everyone about Sabine's stand against the soldiers.

Papa was proud of Sabine. "Ha! You gave them a dose of their own medicine."

But Mama scolded her. "Don't repeat such foolish acts. You draw attention to yourself."

Sabine didn't know if Katana's feather was magic, but it had certainly changed her. She would always speak up against injustice. That was the only way to deal with soldiers cooking up new laws. But Zena's discomfort nagged at Sabine like mango fibres trapped between her teeth.

All week there was no news of Uncle. Each day lasted forever, reminding Sabine of the decrepit midnight train she once took from Nairobi to Mombasa. Bapa had taken her on the trip to show her the railroad tracks he had laid when he was a young boy. As the train rumbled ever so slowly through the jungle in pitch darkness, her only thought, over and over, was *Are we there?*

One evening, Papa said the PSU office suggested that the kondos might have attacked Zully to steal his car. Both Sabine and Mama looked at Papa with horror. Armed with razor-sharp machetes, the kondos didn't just steal. They chopped off an ear for a pair of earrings, an arm for a watch, a leg for a pair of shoes. The police could never catch them.

Alone in her room, Sabine was overcome by guilt. If only ... if only she had ratted about Butabika! Mama would have forced Uncle to stop driving his flashy sports car.

At school, everything changed. Kampala Academy was one of the best private school for girls in the city. It had been built for the affluent English expatriate families. All the past headmasters of the school had been mzungus; the photographs of their stern, white faces lined the hallway. Now the government enforced an Africanization policy by appointing an African headmaster.

French and Latin classes were struck off and replaced with Swahili. Sabine was glad about that, anyway—soon she would be able to converse fluently in Swahili with Zena and Katana.

The O-Lord prayer recited every morning was replaced by the national anthem, but few students knew the words. Sabine was asked to lead the school assembly.

"Oh Uganda! May God uphold thee," she sang with pride, enjoying the projection of her voice through the microphone. "We lay our future in thy hand. United, free, for liberty. Together we'll always stand ..."

The horrified parents of the children who attended the school called a series of meetings to protest, but that fell on deaf ears.

At home, too, everything changed. Munchkin threw

more tantrums than before. And the tension between their parents sizzled like drops of water on hot oil as they fought over insignificant things. Sabine spent most of her time roosting at Paradise Place in the backyard.

What she hated most were the nights. They stretched on forever. Every night she heard the discordant voices of her parents and tried to muffle the sounds with her pillow. Questions churned in her head. Was Uncle safe? Was he a prisoner? Did he get to eat? Where did he sleep? Did he miss his lollipops?

When Sabine returned from school on Friday, she was surprised to see so many cars parked outside their house. Inside, the rooms reeked of perfume. Mama's friends had come in droves to express their grief at Uncle's disappearance.

Sabine knew these pompous china-doll ladies in their fluorescent makeup. They often came over to drink chai. She would hear them complain and bicker about their lazy servants, or *boi*, as they called them. But when their boi left to visit their families in their villages, these ladies ran amok like headless chickens.

Sabine saw that the ladies had staked out a place in the sitting room. They sat cross-legged on the carpet, clicking *tasbhi* beads and singing devotional *bhajans* as if they were attending a funeral ceremony.

"So sorry," the ladies told Mama with sorrow-stricken faces.

"Zully will be missed."

"What will we do without Zully Passport?"

Sabine's stare collided with the dead-fish eyes of the ladies. She had to chase them out. The mourning was killing her mother's hopes. The ladies seemed more concerned about their immigration problems than they were about Uncle. Only Lalita proved helpful. She tried to restrain Munchkin, who adored the attention and pity-filled pats from the ladies.

Mama told Katana to serve chai and biscuits to the visitors.

Sabine glared. *This is no tea party. Stop your useless chatter. Go home! We'll find Uncle. We will, we will.* Enough, she decided.

"Mama, you need to rest," said Sabine loudly.

Mama thanked the ladies, who exchanged glances among themselves, and before long they were all gone.

That evening Papa came home with a smile as bright as the full moon.

"Guli, Sabine, the police found Zully's car!"

Uncle's car had turned up in one of the parking lots adjacent to Entebbe Airport. There was no evidence of a struggle. So Uncle had not met with an accident, and the kondos had not attacked him. The muffler in Uncle's car roared in Sabine's mind. The roaring mingled with Uncle's deep belly laugh, and her heart whooped. Uncle could not be far from them. Papa's political connections had finally paid off. She looked up at him in admiration.

"But where is Zully?" said Mama, looking more fearful than before.

"The police are still looking for him," said Papa. "They will check the passenger lists for all the departures from the airport."

"Did they search Uncle's car? Is there a note or something?" asked Sabine.

Papa shook his head. "The car's spanking clean. Not a single blood cell. The police are checking the fingerprints."

Questions threatened to deflate Sabine's new euphoria. Why did Uncle go to the airport? Was he running away from something or someone? Did he take a flight? If so, where to? Why didn't he call? She loved mysteries, but only in books.

Later, when Mama was upstairs putting Munchkin to bed, Sabine decided to break her pact with Uncle. Only some parts. After all, the information might help Papa find Uncle. Papa listened intently to her. His jaw tightened when she told him about Butabika.

"Zully may have run afoul of the One-Elevens." Papa rubbed his face and thought for a few moments. He put his arm around Sabine. "I'll try another route to find him. Don't worry. We'll find him soon."

Sabine nodded. The decrepit midnight train she felt she had boarded at the beginning of the week had pulled out of the jungle at last, but as it rumbled across the thorny scrubland of the Tsavo plains, herds of gazelles, zebras, antelopes, and even the lazy hippo in the swamp ran to watch the caterpillar creature crawl on rails in the dark. Slow, perhaps, but Sabine was determined to reach her destination as long as the train did not crash or derail or run out of track.

— In the Park —

It was Sunday and Zena was coming over. Sabine kicked off her shoes and peeled off her socks. She slipped on her sandals. She would have to be cautious after their fight over Lalita last week. But it was only a difference of opinion, she thought, nothing else.

She would make a friendship bracelet for Zena, the kind she'd learned to make in art class at school. She found the twine in the craft box. She cut three strands about a metre in length and twisted the ends into a tight overhand knot. She went on weaving and pulling the knots tight. It was quiet. Katana was at his village. Papa, Mama, and Munchkin had gone with Lalita to the airport to drop off her husband, Viram Uncle, who was leaving for India.

The bracelet looked bright. Sabine was pleased. Then she set out tall glasses of lemonade and a plate of flaky bowtie biscuits, the ones Zena liked. Everything had to be perfect. She heard a car on the driveway and ran to the door.

A military jeep had pulled up. Quickly she hid behind the brocade curtains of the sitting room and watched.

Captain Asafa had brought Zena in the jeep. Sadness swept over Sabine. It was just like how Uncle used to drive her in his sports car.

The Captain climbed out of the jeep and Sabine's skin crawled. The tall, stately figure looked severe, so different from his round, cheerful sister, Aunty Halima, at Bapa's farm. Was it the gun in his holster that heightened her fears?

Zena stepped out of the jeep and kissed the Captain. She wore the same kanga pantsuit as she had last Sunday, and her beaded braids tumbled down to her shoulders. The Captain glanced at their house, waved at Zena, and took off.

Sabine ran to the door. "They found Uncle's car."

"Wonderful!" said Zena, and they hugged each other. "Dada's government has brought in good tidings. Soon they'll trace your uncle," said Zena. "Good things have blown our way as well. Uncle's been promoted. They even gave him the jeep to use at his disposal."

"Great!" said Sabine, relieved there were no remnants of their conflict last week. She led Zena inside and showed her the bracelet. She tied it around Zena's wrist.

"It's lovely! It matches my beads." Zena held up her beaded braids.

"Can you braid my hair too?" Sabine found some beads in the craft box.

"Later," said Zena, and Sabine slipped the beads into her pocket.

They drank the lemonade and ate the biscuits. Zena walked behind the glass cabinet to the models of the Taj Mahal and Big Ben from Papa's travels, admiring them as if she were seeing them for the first time. She walked to the alcove on the far right and peeped through the French doors.

"That's Papa's office," said Sabine.

"Interesting," said Zena.

They went upstairs to Sabine's room to practise their dance. Except for a few missteps, they performed very well.

"Let's go to the park," suggested Sabine afterward, feeling she'd been cooped up inside for too long.

They went to get the bikes. The steel frame of Sabine's new bicycle shone in the noon sun, making the red sprockets on the wheels sparkle like rubies.

"You can ride my Cyclone," she said to Zena, bringing the new bike over to her. Zena looked pleased as she mounted it, checked the smoothly shifting gears, and rode out of the yard.

Sabine got on her old bike and pedalled hard after Zena. They rode along the jacaranda-lined road, heads bent, hair flapping. At the park, they left their bikes near the playground. Some Indian children on the swings and slides stared at them. Sabine was glad that none of her classmates were around.

The girls sprawled on the sun-soaked field speckled with dandelions. A warm breeze caressed Sabine's face, and she closed her eyes for a moment to take in the scent of wildflowers. Red-breasted robins and blue bullfinches sang and butterflies flitted from flower to flower. She dreamt they were in Kasenda.

The dream shattered.

"Some people are born lucky," Zena said wistfully, eyeing Sabine's bikes. "I will have to make my luck."

"I'm Wednesday's child," blurted Sabine. "'Wednesday's child is born with bags of money,'" she added, quoting a Gujarati saying.

"Then Friday's child must be born with rocks." Zena's voice crackled like mustard seeds popping in hot ghee.

"Oh! It's a silly old saying my papa told me once," said Sabine, regretting having brought it up.

"You'll be rich. You'll inherit all your family's businesses."

"Uh-huh," said Sabine.

Zena's brow rose. "How will you run Bapa's farms?"

"Oh, there's Aunty Halima, the workers, Ssekore. You will help, won't you?"

"I'm not a *shamba* girl." Zena sat up. "I'm not picking coffee beans all my life." She tugged at a clump of weeds, roots and all. "I want to be rich and famous. My uncle said he'd help me." Her rosebud lips curled. She uprooted a few more weeds.

"Don't do that," said Sabine.

"Why?"

Sabine looked at the sunny bits of dandelion flowers in Zena's dark hands and shrugged.

"They're just weeds." Zena threw them.

Sabine bit her lip. "I know." Things between her and Zena were as slippery as banana peels. Zena yanked out another clump of weeds furiously, and then another. Soon there would be none left in the park, Sabine thought.

After a few long minutes, Sabine said, "School's boring. We don't do a thing." She groaned. "Most of my teachers are new. The old ones were expatriates and have left."

"I've got tons of work," said Zena. "Plus the house chores. They never end."

Zena's public school was not affected by the expulsion, as her teachers were Africans. Sabine's hand in her pocket felt the beads, and she took them out for her braids. But before she could ask, Zena intercepted.

"I can't. Your hair's too soft and silky for braids."

"Oh!" said Sabine, disappointed. Zena must be angry with her. She used to braid her hair in Kasenda.

"Oh, well, I'll try." Zena dragged herself behind Sabine. She divided Sabine's hair into little sections.

Silence reigned for a while, the girls lost in their own thoughts.

In Kasenda, Zena always massaged Sabine's head first. Sabine loved the pressure of her friend's firm fingertips kneading and loosening the tension bumps. Today, though, Zena was acting weird. Was she still upset about the incident over Lalita?

"Uncle Asafa has big plans for me," said Zena.

"Uh-huh," said Sabine, worried about saying the wrong thing.

"You know, girls in my tribe marry young," said Zena.

"Uh-huh," said Sabine again. Zena was a year and a half older than Sabine, almost seventeen.

"Uncle's trying to arrange my marriage." Zena had finished the first braid down to the nape of her neck. She picked a bead from Sabine's palm and threaded it into the braid. "He wants me to marry a high-ranking official in the army."

Sabine's jaw fell open. She was glad Zena could not see her face.

"What about you?" asked Zena.

"Me?" The beads in Sabine's palm rolled and clicked against each other, pushing a bead over the edge onto the grass. "I want to go to college first." She didn't want to be an ordinary housewife like Mama.

"I don't think your father would allow you to marry a man from another community."

"Oh! Don't be silly." Sabine retrieved the bead. She knew quite well that Zena had a point. Indians kept to themselves; cross-marriage even within the different Indian communities was frowned upon. But she didn't want to think about it. Not right now.

They fell quiet. Sabine felt a yank and a twist each time a new section of her hair was braided. Soon Zena threaded the last bead and dragged herself forward to sit next to Sabine.

"Thanks." Sabine tossed her head and glanced sideways to see her beaded braids fly into the arc of a rainbow. She wished Ssekore could see her.

"Sabine ... I know all about your father," said Zena.

"Papa? What about Papa?"

"Never mind."

"Never mind what?"

"You won't like it."

"What won't I like?" Sabine shook Zena's arm. "Tell me."

Zena drew her legs up protectively so her knees touched her chin and her arms were wrapped around them. "My uncle said your father's a loan shark."

"He's not!" Sabine glared at Zena. "You can't say things like that about my father."

"Told you you wouldn't like it." Zena threw up her hands. "I'm telling you because you're my friend. If you don't want me to, I won't say anything."

"Zena, people love Papa. When the visitors come to see Papa they bring presents, a live chicken, brown eggs, or soda bottles filled with fresh goat milk."

"They give gifts because they can't repay their loans in time. And when they can't, the interest on the loan doubles."

"But ..." The blue of the sky seemed to close in on Sabine, and she felt the air around her grow thin.

"The debt becomes bigger and bigger," said Zena. "The poor can never repay it."

"Your uncle's wrong. Papa lends the money from the goodness of his heart."

"Forget it," snapped Zena.

How could Sabine forget it? She wanted to shake Zena like a rag doll. "You don't know Papa. It's a lie." She slapped the dirt off her pants and rose.

Zena rose as well. "Want to play on the swings?"

"I'm tired," said Sabine. *Papa is not a loan shark.* "Let's go."

They walked over to the bicycles, but Zena refused to ride the Cyclone.

"Fine, use my old bike," said Sabine. Zena was plainly jealous.

They rode home in silence. Sabine's limbs were leaden, and it was a struggle to pedal the Cyclone. At every turn of the wheel Zena's accusation rang in Sabine's head and her muscles screamed in agony. She felt as if she was riding up a steep slope.

They parted politely, like strangers.

— Papa's Office —

Was Papa a loan shark? Sabine felt as if the heavy grind-stone in which Katana sometimes pounded the curry spices hung around her neck.

On Monday afternoon she got the opportunity she had been waiting for. She was alone. Papa was at work, Mama and Munchkin had gone with Mzee, their driver, to visit friends for tea, and Katana had escaped to read outside.

Sabine found the keys to Papa's office in the key rack. Not only was the room private, it was locked as well. She turned the key and the French doors swung open.

She saw something stirring on the wall—the tail of the lion rug—and screamed, only to realize that the movement was an illusion: opening the door wider made the light reflect differently. Strange—she hadn't seen the rug last time, when she was in the office with Papa.

Her head throbbed with a fearful expectancy as she looked around. She stepped cautiously toward the rosewood desk. Her gaze fell on the Tree of Life, and a funny sensation stirred in her throat, a feeling of guilt and intrusion. She shook it off. *I am only investigating to clear Papa's name.* She had to be quick. Someone was bound to come home soon.

She sat on Papa's high-backed leather chair and pulled open the drawers, rummaging inside, examining the contents carefully—pens, pencils, papers, restaurant receipts, stamps. She continued searching, checking every drawer. Passports, documents, a stack of letters, more pens, pencils, paper.

She pulled out a thick brown envelope and looked inside. A stack of photos. She looked at them briefly. Most photos were of the farm workers; one showed Bapa and Aunty Halima. Sabine was wasting time. Zena was wrong about Papa. There was nothing suspicious here.

Sabine's gaze fell on the brass-studded Zanzibar curio chest lying sedately in the corner. Was it a treasure chest? Her detective mind was turning too fanciful, the result of reading too many thrillers and seeing James Bond movies with Uncle.

She knelt on the floor and examined the chest. In the silence she could hear her heart tick louder than the wall clock. She lifted the lid.

Files, folders, a stack of letters, a copy of the Koran, and a House of Manji biscuit tin. Why would Papa keep a biscuit tin here? The tin was heavy. Gold ingots? Her hands broke out in a sweat as she lifted the lid off. The tin was filled to the brim with chocolate biscuits. *Aha,* she said to herself, smiling, as she lifted the wax paper under the biscuits to see the layer underneath.

There were stacks of hundred-shilling bills neatly bundled in elastic bands. She stared at them, her breath caught in her throat for a fleeting moment. Was this the money Papa loaned out? She felt like a stone that had been dropped into a well, falling down, down, deeper, deeper.

She wiped her sweaty hands on her pants, rose, and left the office. She locked the French doors behind her and shuffled to the sitting room, peeking through the window, watching out for Papa, bracing herself to confront him. Long ago, when she was little, she'd wait at this very window for Papa, and when he came, he'd swing her up onto his shoulders and she'd shriek until Mama pleaded with him to stop.

At last she saw Papa's car pull up the driveway, and ran to the door.

Papa set his leather briefcase down. "How's my boy?"

"Very well, thank you," she said, waiting as he took off his shiny black loafers. Then she pulled his arm. "Papa."

"Yes, dear." He ruffled her hair and kissed her.

"Why do you hide money in a biscuit tin?"

"Snooping around, eh?" He wiggled her nose and laughed. "My dear, you know Kampala is rampant with kondos. The hidden money is bait. It is a red herring to divert the thieves from harming us." He loosened his tie.

But Sabine was not done. "Papa, do you give out loans?"

He straightened. "Who told you that?" He pulled at the hairs on his mustache.

"Papa, it's not right."

"Sabine, you know my business is marketing and exporting crops from our farms. But the poor farm workers who know me well sometimes come to me for help.

— 87 —

They need cash for fertilizer, bride price, or school fees. Banks won't lend them money because they have no assets. What can they do?"

"You charge them interest?"

"To cover bad debts. Sometimes they can't repay the loan."

Sabine exhaled. She felt lighter. The grindstone that had been strapped around her neck for three days was lifted. Zena was wrong. Papa was only helping the poor. Without the loan, what would the poor farmers do? How would their children go to school?

She pulled Papa down and pecked his prickly cheek. Papa was not a loan shark.

— At Zena's —

September 10, 1972

DAY 36

All week there was no news of Uncle. Finally it was Sunday, and Sabine was on her way to Zena's, determined to clear her father's name.

Sabine sat in the back seat of the car behind Mzee, twirling a lock of chestnut hair around her finger. No new facts had emerged since Uncle's car was found, and now other people were reported as missing—a journalist, a professor at Makerere University, and the Chief Justice. Sabine could not understand how they, like Uncle, had disappeared without a trace. As if a wicked *djinn* had whisked them away on a magic carpet. *Zoom.*

Papa said men who vanished mysteriously might have challenged the government; Katana said the disappearance was tribal-related. Katana was a Langi, the same tribe as ex-President Obote, and there was a lot of tension between the current President Amin's men and Obote's men. Well, tribal strife was common, as the colonials had ignored the tribal kingdoms and carved up Africa like a pie. Thankfully, Uncle didn't care for politics, nor was he a Langi.

Sabine thanked Mzee for the ride and climbed out of the car. The path wound around the cluster of papaya and matoke trees. The sky was overcast with a slight breeze. Katana had dreamt of red snakes last night and predicted that it would rain today, but Sabine refused to take an umbrella with her. She was sure the sun would shine. Sundays were always sunny. She turned in at the last row of flats and slowed as she caught a glimpse of the tall Captain talking to Zena in the compound.

Sabine hid behind a tree and watched furtively. Why was Zena carrying a washbasin of clothes? Her usual washday was Friday. The Captain's hands were clasped behind his back while Zena caught the hems of her long skirt and looked down at her bare feet. As the Captain talked to Zena, she fingered the string of shiny cowry shells around her neck. Were they having a fight? Then he hugged Zena and disappeared behind the closed door of their flat.

Sabine stepped out of her spot, ducked under the clothesline, and ran across the cement compound.

Zena smiled weakly at Sabine, then bunched up her skirt and squatted by the cistern in the communal wash area shared by the residents of Block H.

The wash area made Sabine squeamish. Usually the residents of the flats washed their pots or clothes here, but last week she had seen the Chicken Man twist the neck of a clucking hen before he invoked the name of Allah and slaughtered it with his knife. The wash area had been filled with blood and scattered chicken parts.

"We can't meet," Zena said softly, without looking up. She sorted through a pile of laundry, her beaded braids spilling over her face.

"I'll wait. You can finish your washing." Sabine looked around to check if Ssekore was around.

"Ssekore's moved in with his friend in Mengo," said Zena, as if reading Sabine's mind. She rubbed the blue cake of soap on her uncle's military shirt.

The sight of the shirt assaulted Sabine's senses and built pressure in her head.

"Sabine, you have to leave."

The words hung in the space between them.

Sabine's hands dropped at her sides like dead weights. "Aren't we going to practise our dance?"

"It's cancelled." Zena turned on the tap and filled the basin with fresh water. She rinsed the shirt in it. The water clouded with soap scum, and dirty suds rose to the top.

"But ..." Sabine's tongue flopped uselessly in her mouth.

Overhead, the sun surrendered to a cloud. Sabine dropped to her knees to be on the same level as her friend, her pale fists digging into her thighs.

"I don't understand."

"You won't." Zena's rosebud lips twisted. She wrung the shirt with both hands. She still wore the friendship bracelet around her wrist. "Uncle's been promoted. We have to be careful," she said, glancing over her shoulder at her flat.

Sabine followed Zena's gaze and saw the tall silhouette of the Captain in the kitchen window. It was his fault. She hated, hated, hated soldiers. But Zena loved her uncle as much as Sabine loved Uncle Lollipop.

"I'm sorry. Dada Amin's orders. We cannot associate with Indians."

"But we are Ugandans."

"You are Indian, I'm African."

"I'm African too. Indo-African."

"You are brown. I'm black."

Pain sank into the cavities of Sabine's innermost organs. It's not fair, she thought. The Africans didn't understand Indians and the Indians didn't understand Africans. Their communities had plunged her and Zena apart and destroyed their friendship.

She tried a lighter note. "I can look like you." Once in Kasenda she used black shoe polish to camouflage her face in the dark while playing hide-and-seek, and everyone had a good laugh.

Zena didn't even smile. She picked up a stone and attacked a towel, beating on it. *Thud, thud.* Sabine's heart beat in unison, and in between the thuds, in the silence of unspoken words, she heard the wind and the rustling of scraps of newspaper. Somewhere inside one of the flats, a baby wailed. A mother yelled through an open window for her child to come inside.

Zena rinsed the towel in clean water, then wrung it with both hands.

Sabine jerked as she caught a spray of cold sprinkles.

"Sorry," said Zena. She drained the dirty water inside the basin, and Sabine felt dirty and discarded as well. Zena carried the basin of clothes to the clothes-line. Sabine followed her, watching as Zena put down the basin and began to hang the clothes and peg them to the clothesline.

"Soon there will be school holidays and we will be in Kasenda."

Zena turned sharply. "I don't want to come and be your worker."

"You don't have to."

"My children will work under you. Their children will work for your children and so on. I must break this cycle or we'll always be your slaves."

"Zena, if you knew …"

"I know," she said. "I have to treat you like a princess, a *memsahib*. Your family is special. Always it was I who tended the vegetable patch, picked coffee beans, saw to it that you didn't run too far and get lost."

Sabine folded her arms to steady herself. "You've joined them?"

"Them? Them are us. Your people have clogged up our land as the British *bwanas* did before. Your people, your family included, are doing magendo, illegal activities."

"Uncle and Papa help people out of kindness."

"We don't want kindness." Zena gave a short, dry laugh. "You took our land and made us look after it. Now we want it back."

Sabine stared at Zena. But Bapa had bought the land and cleared it to grow coffee.

"We have to clear our land," Zena continued. "The weeds must be uprooted. What can I do? You are the child of dandelions."

Sabine reeled as if struck by lightning. How dare Zena accuse her of being a weed? What insolence! *I am not your dirty laundry.* If Zena wanted to act smart and saucy, the loss would be hers. Zena needed her more than she needed Zena. She would come around in time. *I will not stand like a dumb cabbage head and take it from a poor African with an attitude.* She raised her chin, gave a scornful laugh, and huffed away. When she glanced back, she saw that Zena, cradling the empty basin in the crook of her arm, was leaving as well.

Sabine felt a tremor in her legs. The tremor grew. The earth shifted under her feet. She sank onto the flagstone in the compound. The sky had darkened and a light rain began to fall. But Zena did not come out to get her laundry. When it rained in Kasenda, she and Zena did the rain dance to express their gratitude to the gods. They whirled in their bare feet, their heads tipped up to the sky, open mouths taking the raindrops as the red mud turned their feet red.

We were twin beans of one coffee flower. We did everything together. Sabine's Bapa was their Bapa and Zena's Aunty Halima was Sabine's aunty. When Zena did the housekeeping chores for Aunty Halima, Sabine helped peel potatoes and carrots, shell peas, clean the rice, so Zena would be let off early. Had she forgotten that?

Sabine's eyes closed momentarily, and she saw herself and Zena chasing butterflies one dog-hot afternoon.

"Let's plant friendship seeds," Zena said. *"Our friendship tree will grow."*

We planted the coffee beans.

"*Friends forever,*" *said Zena.*

"*Forever and ever,*" *I said.*

In her room Sabine had a photo of them in front of their coffee bush. The bush had grown, and soon the bush would blossom.

Her wild hair flew askew, whirling around her head like snakes. The wind seemed to have gathered a sudden strength. It flapped the clothes on the clothesline with slapping sounds. She could smell the freshness of the clothes as they billowed in the breeze. Zena had taken their memories of good times, rubbed, scrubbed, drained, and discarded them.

She looked at Zena's flat one last time and said, "I am not a weed."

The closed door stared back at her.

— Mengo —

Sabine climbed into the back seat of the car, and Mzee pulled away from Zena's flat. Big, fat raindrops pelted the rooftop of their car, the sounds like the juicy plop of ripe fruit dropping from the papaya trees around them. Sabine watched the squeaking wipers on the windshield as they slapped the rain back and forth and struggled to clear the glass. She felt totally disjointed. Broken into pieces. Shattered by pain, so much pain. No amount of rain would wash it away.

What if Zena never called her again? Sabine should have made Zena understand that what other people thought didn't matter to their friendship. What would she do now?

The tin shanties on Mengo Hill came into view. Sabine watched as the smoke rose over the hill and curled up into the hazy sky. Zena said that Ssekore had moved in with his friends in Mengo. Perhaps he would patch up their conflict. She would ask him.

Sabine leaned forward in the seat. "Mzee, can you stop at Mengo."

He turned to look back at her, his gaze downcast out of respect, but she saw the uneasiness on his face, the corners of his mouth twitching. "Mengo, Missy?"

"Yes, please," said Sabine.

"Bwana Sadru will be angry."

"No, no, he won't. Please, for a few minutes only."

He nodded, but reluctantly, it seemed to her.

As the car climbed Mengo hill, doubts invaded Sabine's mind. What if Ssekore shunned her as well? Would he? He did like her, didn't he?

She recalled the last holiday at Kasenda farm, when they talked about fate and fortune.

"A potato plant will not grow grapes," said Zena. "Our fate depends on the shoes our father wore. A chief's son will be a chief," she said, "and a king's son a king. We can't break this cycle."

Ssekore disagreed. "Father drank; I don't. Father didn't go to school. I ..."

"Yes, but will you ever be king?" scoffed Zena.

Ssekore nodded. "I can, if I want to."

"Really?" Zena's voice dripped with sarcasm. "And how, may I ask?"

He glanced at Sabine and winked. "By marrying a queen," he said.

"Silly," Zena said. "That would only make you a duke."

The rain tapered off as the car bumped along the rutty terrain, splashing muddy water in the puddles. Mzee parked the car and glanced uneasily over his shoulder, scouting the vicinity through his window. He turned to Sabine in the back seat but still did not meet her gaze. "Missy," he said, "I come with you."

"Thank you," she said, impulsively touching his arm. He pulled his arm back immediately.

Sabine realized she had never touched Mzee before. She and her family were no different from the standoffish whites and other Indians who distanced themselves from their African employees. Mzee had worked for Bapa at his farm for many years before he moved to the city to get an easier job and became their driver. With stooped shoulders and cracked skin like rich old leather, he looked as old as Bapa, she thought. She didn't even know his name. All elderly men in Africa are respectfully addressed as Mzee.

Sabine followed Mzee down the sloppy mud path. Her sandals squelched with every step. Rain had churned up the red earth into lumpy clots, and the red rainwater streams made the land appear to be bleeding.

Mzee stopped ahead, waiting for Sabine to catch up.

"Mzee, what's your name?" She looked up at him. His eyes lifted in surprise, and she saw they were gentle and crinkled like Bapa's.

"Mzee Kabugo," he said shyly, returning his gaze downward.

"Do you have family?"

He looked up a little. "Five boys, three girls, thirteen grandchildren."

Sabine bit her lip. After all the years Mzee had worked for them, she thought she knew him, but she didn't. "Mzee, what a big family you have!" she said.

He smiled an unwavering smile, and their eyes locked for a second before he looked away.

They passed rows of kiosks, their roofs covered with bright kanga cloths that said KARIBUNI—WELCOME and I LOVE UGANDA. The kiosks sold everything under the sun: fruits, vegetables, secondhand clothes and shoes, towers of multicoloured plastic tubs, Palmolive soap, Patra perfume, wide-toothed combs, and Ambi cream to lighten skin.

The kiosk owners greeted Mzee and gazed at Sabine with curiosity. Never had Sabine felt so visible, so freakish. She greeted them and they smiled shyly.

"Missy, the homes are farther," Mzee said, pointing across the field, and Sabine nodded.

Along the way, Sabine asked Mzee why he was working at his age.

Mzee did not reply. He seemed absorbed as he watched a few naked children play on the field. Sabine thought perhaps he hadn't heard her.

Then he spoke. "I am saving to have water piped at home." He paused before continuing. "The well is almost two kilometres away."

The saliva in Sabine's throat stuck like a fishbone, but she managed to nod. If she wanted water at home, all she had to do was to turn on the tap.

The boys ran past them, shrieking as they chased rusty bicycle-wheel rims. Sabine could not help but stare at the children's stick legs and protruding stomachs. She felt the blistering sting of shame. Mama always quarreled with her about not finishing her meals.

One little boy stopped and called out, "Nicey madam, nicey, nicey."

Sabine waved at him and followed Mzee quietly. The air was humid and sticky. They dodged several clucking chickens underfoot, scrabbling for food bits in the dirt, and passed a grass field where women and children squatted around a charcoal-burning stove, cooking and chatting. Some sat on little stools under acacia trees, straightening or braiding their hair.

Mzee stopped and gestured with his hand that they had arrived.

Sabine stared.

Covering the landscape were rows upon rows of tin and plastic shacks all the way to the horizon over the hilly slope. The shacks huddled together, drawing warmth from each other on this bleak day. She recalled the dwellings of the workers in Kasenda. From Bapa's house, the workers' mud huts stuck out like brown pustules in the rolling green land. It had never bothered her because she had never seen the huts up close.

The stench from a sewage-filled creek hit her, and she felt her stomach move with nausea. How could Ssekore or anyone else live here? Her head buzzed like the cloud of black flies over the rotting food scraps at her feet. She didn't belong. She was an alien, an extraterrestrial being from the planet of Nakasero, who had intruded upon them.

No wonder they couldn't wait to take over the homes, shops, and farms of the rich Indians! She stood gazing at the wet tin shacks and understood suddenly, dizzyingly, something else as well: that her friendship with Ssekore would hit a dead end. When Zena asked at the park about intermarriage, Sabine had lied. It *was* taboo in Indian culture to have a relationship with a black African. And what if he, like Zena, had changed? She would rather hold on to her memory of the boy she had once liked, and who had once liked her, than risk learning the answer.

"Mzee, let's leave." Sabine linked her arm through his.

He looked startled and opened his mouth to say something, then didn't.

They returned to the car quietly, and this time Sabine sat in the front seat beside Mzee. As they pulled away from Mengo, she felt relieved to see the tin shanties shrink farther and farther into the distance.

Back at home, Sabine ran to her room and locked the door. She didn't want to tell Papa or Mama or anyone about Zena. How could Zena dump her? It was humiliating, a slap to her face. Munchkin thumped on her door, but she didn't budge.

The hole made by Uncle's disappearance grew deeper and darker, a yawning fissure, a chasm as wide as the Great Rift Valley of East Africa. A flood of tears flowed with such passion that it felt like the Owen Falls Dam had burst. She didn't know if she was crying because her crush on Ssekore had died or because Zena had spurned her or because Uncle was still missing.

When she could cry no more, she resolved to get back at Zena. Friendship was not a football to be tossed around and kicked. If Zena called her to make up, Sabine would not give in easily. *I don't trust you, Zena,* she'd say. Let Zena's blackberry eyes flutter. Sabine would make Zena feel so guilty that never again would Zena spurn her. *Zena, broken hearts can be glued back, but the cracks will always be there.*

— The Breakdown —

Sabine waited for Zena to contact her. Monday morning, afternoon, evening, Tuesday morning, afternoon ... but she never called. Sabine's mind replayed clips of every place she had been with Zena and the secrets they had shared. She missed Zena with every fibre of her being. Didn't Zena miss her at all?

Meanwhile, horror struck Kampala when Mr. Madhvani, an Indian businessman, was arrested. To any Ugandan, the name Madhvani conjured images of luxurious mansions, expensive cars, jets, and lots of cash. The radio, newspapers, and the evening television reported his arrest, but no reason was given.

After supper on Tuesday, Sabine joined her family in the sitting room. Mama sat with Munchkin on her lap watching cartoons on television, her fingers intertwining, then coming apart. Papa, in his armchair, read the newspaper splashed with pictures of Mr. Madhvani.

"Fool!" Papa's lips twisted in a sneer at the President's action. Papa said that Mr. Madhvani owned so many industries that he controlled Uganda's economy. "Uganda cannot exist without Madhvani! Why would that clown arrest him?"

"I know why," Mama said softly.

Both Sabine and Papa looked at Mama in surprise.

"Lalita told me that Mr. Madhvani's daughter-in-law, Mumtaz, turned down the President's invitation for an evening of pleasure," Mama explained.

Sabine was appalled by the President's overture. She had a poster of Mumtaz in her room. The beautiful actress was the heartthrob of all Indian men and envied by women. Then it struck Sabine that the gossip was probably a rumour. To Lalita's ears, gossip was as sweet and sticky as halva.

"Mama, that is just a rumour," said Sabine.

Mama didn't respond. Either she didn't hear Sabine or she chose not to hear. Her gaze was fixed on Papa, her face scrunched in distress. "Sadru, the fire's spreading, burning rich Indian businessmen," she said, wringing her hands as if squeezing out her anxiety.

"Enough!" Papa rose. He stared down at Mama. "We've been through this many times, Guli. There is no safe haven on earth." He kept on staring at Mama, his upper lip and mustache bristling.

Sabine wrapped her arms around herself. She wished her parents would stop fighting over other people's problems and come up with new ways to find Uncle.

Over the following days, the countdown infiltrated their home and extinguished all signs of life. Dead days crawled by, days when the brocade curtains in their sitting room remained drawn and Gandhi, in the gilded portrait on the wall, pouted. Papa was always away meeting new government officials. Mama stayed in bed more and more. Katana's stories and songs stopped as he spent his time in the backyard, his head buried in Sabine's old books. Even Munchkin's gurgles sounded flat. And there was no word from Zena.

Sabine came home from school to find the house so quiet that she could hear the walls moan and groan. Today was Uncle's birthday. Last year they celebrated his birthday at Sweety Sweets and then went to Sno Cream for double scoops of chocolate ice cream.

She dumped her satchel on the kitchen counter. She found Mama on the floor in the sitting room, looking through Uncle's photo album. Munchkin, at her side, had his scrapbook of wild animals on his lap. It was filled with the cards that Sabine had collected for him from Brooke Bond tea packets.

She hugged and kissed her brother.

"Eeeee!" He pushed his scrapbook at her.

"Okay," she said, turning the pages quickly.

When Munchkin was absorbed in his scrapbook again, Sabine pulled herself closer to Mama so she could see Uncle's album. Most of the photos were of Uncle taking part in the Safari Car Rally. Drivers from all over the world took part in this three-day gruelling rally through the rugged terrain of the three countries of East Africa. Many drivers were forced out of the rally, but Uncle was always one of the top ten drivers.

In one photo, Uncle looked very proud as he held up a

trophy he had won in the rally. Sabine recalled the fawning fans cheering him—*Zull-y, Zull-y, Zull-y*—as his car raced past the Kampala checkpoint.

Mama looked at the photograph, her eyes filled with longing. "Zully was so mischievous," she said. "When he was as young as Minaz, I would wash his hair, and he'd shake his wet head to throw cold sprinkles at me. He would have been thirty today."

Would have? Sabine flared up. "Mama, why are you talking in the past tense?"

"It's kismet, dear. We can't fight fate."

Sabine sprang forward as if to resist her mother's submissive and defeatist attitude, which seemed to push her deeper into the hole that had opened up with Uncle's disappearance. "We can, Mama! We must. We have to!"

They stared at each other, waging a silent eye war. In a while, Mama blinked.

"Uncle is alive," Sabine asserted. "I know he is."

Mama shook her head slowly.

The denial cut the threads of Sabine's hope. Anger jumped out of her throat like a bolt of lightning. "No, no, no!" she yelled again and again.

She couldn't help herself. She was mad at Mama for giving up hope so easily. She was mad at Zena for not apologizing or even bothering to call. She was mad about how long it was taking to find Uncle. The anger expanded inside her. She felt that her chest wall might explode. She got up. She kicked the stool as hard as she could. It hit the wall—*bang!*—and then fell onto the floor with a broken leg.

Mama's hands flew to cover her face, and she began to sob uncontrollably.

"Eeeeeee!" Munchkin bawled as well.

Now what? Sabine looked at the broken stool and couldn't believe that she had lost control. It wasn't just the stool—*everything* was falling apart. She had to take charge. Papa would be terribly disappointed in her. She swallowed. She must conserve her energy. Her bigger battle was to fight the soldiers.

She took out Uncle's model car from her satchel and gave it to Munchkin to play with, and he quieted. She helped Mama onto the sofa.

She held her mother's hand. "I'm sorry, Mama," she said softly. "But we can't give up! We can't let the soldiers win!"

She called for Katana, who bobbed in at once as if he had been waiting at the door. "Boil some saffron milk for Mama and some Milo for Minazi."

"Yes," said Katana, and he disappeared into the kitchen.

Soon the house filled up with the sweet scent of cardamom. Sabine gave a cup of steaming saffron milk to Mama, but she put it on the table. So Sabine held the cup to Mama's lips while Katana helped Munchkin with his Milo. In a while she saw the colour return to her mother's cheeks. "Mama, you need to lie down," she said. She told Katana to look after Munchkin and helped her mother upstairs to her room.

They sat on the bed. "Thank you, dear," said Mama,

her petal-soft hands stroking Sabine's face, tracing the outlines of her nose, cheeks, down to her dimpled chin. "I'm sorry. You are close to Zully. It must be so hard for you. I'm not making it any easier."

"It's not your fault, Mama," said Sabine, catching a tear at the corner of her eye. "I know how you feel. I'd feel the same if anything were to happen to Munchkin." She kissed her mother on the forehead and smelled her rose scent blending with the salt of her tears. "Don't worry, Mama. If Papa cannot find Uncle, I will."

—— War Days ——

Sabine felt too heavy to get up. Sunday had turned into the worst day of the week, when the ghosts of the past haunted her. Her mind flitted from Zena to Uncle. She took out his model car from under her pillow and opened and closed the hood repeatedly. Clearly, Papa's efforts at finding Uncle had not worked. Time was slipping by. She had to take charge. How? What should she do? What could she do?

The radio on her night table crackled with static. Instead of the stupid countdown, the newsman said, "Tanzania is at war with us. They must stop interfering in our internal matters. Fellow Ugandans, be brave and loyal."

Sabine bolted downstairs and found Papa reading. "War," she gasped.

Papa folded the paper and pulled her onto the sofa near him. "A minor invasion, dear. Ex-President Obote is trying to regain power, so his men, hiding in Tanzania, have attacked the Ugandan army at the border."

Papa draped his arm around Sabine's shoulders. It held her panic in check, like a paperweight preventing a stack of papers from scattering.

"Anyway, the fighting is internal. It doesn't affect us."

"Of course it does," said Mama, coming from the

kitchen. "Zully's case will be delayed again. And there will be a shortage of food. We must stockpile the essentials."

Mama called Katana and sent him shopping.

"Yes, Mama Guli," he said dutifully, though it was Sunday.

"And tell Mzee to fill the car with petrol," added Papa.

"Yes, Bwana Sadru," said Katana, and left.

Sabine nestled against Papa and buried her head in his chest, content to hear his heartbeats, her head rocking gently to the rhythm of his inhalations and exhalations. The world could fight and scream and cry, but she was safe as long as she was burrowed inside Papa's protective shell.

Sabine was making a tower of wooden blocks for Munchkin when Katana stormed through the front door carrying an armload of groceries. His teeth chattered uncontrollably.

"What happened, Katana?" Sabine took the bags of groceries from his shaking hands and dumped them on the floor, ignoring Munchkin, who ran to peek inside them.

"Ka-ta-na!" Mama yelled as she hurried from the kitchen. She saw him shivering and stopped midway. "What's wrong?"

Katana's eye opened wider. "Mama, the soldiers—they took ... Bwana's Mercedes."

Mama's flour-dusted hands flew over her mouth.

"My car?" Papa put his newspaper down. He sprang up. "Boneheads! Who took my car?"

In one big breath Katana said that he was buying groceries at Uchumi Supermarket, and Mzee was putting petrol in the car, when some soldiers grabbed the car keys from Mzee at gunpoint. They said they urgently needed cars to transport Ugandan soldiers to the Uganda-Tanzania border to fight Obote's men.

"Mzee be sick and go home. Bwana, I be very sorry," he said, breathing hard and sweating profusely.

"It's not your fault," said Papa. He put his arm around Katana and helped him to the sofa. "I'm glad you and Mzee are safe. Mzee can drive Mama's Toyota."

"Katana, you need to rest," said Sabine. He was working on his day off.

"Yes," said Mama and Papa together. "Go. Rest."

Sabine camped with her family in the sitting room for the rest of the day, their ears tuned to the radio for news. She and Papa amused Munchkin, building towers of wooden blocks for him and then letting him knock them down. Mama's lips moved silently as she clicked her amber prayer beads.

At midnight, the radio came to life: "We have bombed the Tanzanian town of Bukoba. We are winning the war. There will be a curfew in effect from dusk to dawn, six p.m. to six a.m. Anybody who breaks the curfew will be shot."

The war marched on for two weeks. Every day the radio played military music; no voices came on to report the countdown; no casualties were reported; no news was reported. Papa did not go to his office, and Sabine did not go to school. Every evening Kampala slipped into darkness and Sabine's life was reduced to dark shapes and shadows.

—

Mama was with Munchkin upstairs and Sabine was playing Monopoly with Papa when the voice on the radio came on. The countdown had awakened from its slumber, Sabine thought. But it was something else. "The President is very happy to inform fellow Ugandans that he is engaged to a beautiful young dancer," the newsman reported.

Sabine looked quizzically at her father. "Papa, why are they talking about the President's engagement to a dancer during a time of war?"

"Because he's a fool with capital *F*." Papa laughed and they resumed playing.

The next day, the newsman announced, "The British have invaded Uganda."

Papa tweaked at his mustache. Then he walked around the house pinching the bridge of his nose, and Sabine felt the tension grow.

Later, the newsman said, "Tanzania is using Chinese experts in the war."

Confused, Sabine looked at Papa, his bushy brows knitted into a frown. He looked out the window, into the darkness, hands clasped behind his back, as if he was looking outside for an answer.

"Papa, is everything okay?"

"Yes, dear." He was smiling, but his voice betrayed him. "I'll call Commissioner Karanja."

Papa spoke to the police commissioner in Luanda, a dialect that Sabine did not understand. She watched Papa's smile dissolve into a stiff expression and bit all her finger-nails down to little nubbins as he talked for what seemed like a long time.

At last Papa put down the receiver, but he kept looking at it. Sabine's raw, pink fingertips throbbed.

"There is no war," he said at last. "Amin is playing games." He looked at the wall, so she turned to look there too, but there was nothing.

"I ... I don't understand."

Papa's jaw tightened. "First he solidified his position, giving his soldiers free shops, houses, and farms left by the British Indians. As Commissioner Karanja says, a dog with a bone in his mouth can't bite you."

"He became their hero," said Sabine, thinking about Zena.

Papa nodded. "The invasion by Obote's troops failed, but now the President wants to eliminate all opposition against him. So he's diverting attention by blaming Tanzania and other countries. Meanwhile his soldiers are killing the Langis, who are loyal to Obote."

Katana was a Langi. Sabine must warn him.

The next day Sabine waited in the kitchen for Katana. The British Indians were lucky, she thought; they were only expelled. But Africans who belonged to the wrong tribe faced death.

As soon as Katana came inside, she asked him about his family and warned him that the soldiers were hunting the Langis.

"I know," he said in a small voice. His eye shut tight for a few silent seconds, then opened again. "You know Juma?"

She nodded. Everyone knew Juma, an old fisherman who went from house to house in Nakasero selling fresh fish.

"Juma fish in the lake near Murchison Falls ..."

Sabine had visited the falls with Uncle. She had counted eight crocodiles in the lake near the falls that day.

"When Juma fish, he get hands and legs."

"Yuck! Katana, fish do not have hands and legs."

"But men do. Crocodile eat some, leave some."

Sabine's neck prickled. Were dead men dumped in the lake? "It's not true."

"I, seventh son of my mother, know." He told her about the "river treatment," when soldiers tied the bodies to cement blocks and dropped them into the Nile, and the "hammer treatment," when they cracked the skulls of prisoners like eggs, and the "helicopter treatment," when they dropped people from a great height.

Sabine refused to be unnerved by the horror stories. She put her hand on his forearm. "Katana, don't listen to rumours." She, too, had heard crazy tales, like one about the President—that he ate the heart of his son because his witch doctor told him that eating the heart of a loved one would protect him from his enemies.

She pulled out the feather from her pocket and pressed it into Katana's palm. "You need the magic more than I do."

She felt for Uncle's model car in her other pocket. That would be her good-luck charm.

— The Detectives —

The gods smiled on Sabine on Saturday. Her prayers for her missing uncle seemed to be answered in the Classified section of the *Uganda Argus* newspaper:

> Private Detective Agency:
> We guarantee to find your missing ones.
> Call Bodyfinders.

The growing number of disappearances had given birth to a new business. Excited, Sabine ran to show the ad to her mother.

"No, dear," said Mama. "It may interfere with Papa's investigation."

Sabine didn't agree, but she didn't argue or check with Papa, who might have refused her as well. If only she and Zena were still friends. Zena would have accompanied her to the agency.

That afternoon, when Mama and Munchkin left to go to Lalita's for tea, Sabine got her chance. She showed Katana the ad and told him of her plan. "Do you know where their office is?" she asked.

Katana checked the address and nodded. "Nsambya

Road by Queen's Clock Tower," he said. He licked his lower lip. "They ask for money."

"I'll pay any amount for my uncle."

His eye blinked rapidly. "You can't go alone. I come with you."

"Thank you," she said, and ran inside. She took some of her savings as well as Uncle's photograph and slipped them in her handbag, and left with Katana and Mzee.

In the car, Sabine heard good news for the first time in a long time. One of Mzee's granddaughters had found a job as a teacher at a private school. Mzee praised Dada Amin for his Africanization policy, and Sabine saw Katana shift uncomfortably in his seat. Mzee said soon they'd be able to pay for running water and he'd retire.

"I am happy for you, Mzee, but I will miss you," said Sabine.

"I, too," he said and added, "Missy, don't forget to invite me to your wedding."

Sabine laughed.

The office of the private detective agency displayed a sign in bold blue letters. BODYFINDERS: DEAD OR ALIVE WE GET THEM FOR YOU.

Two men received Sabine and Katana at the door. One was short, with a round, happy face; the other, tall as a crested crane, looked like a fierce warrior. Both wore leopard-spotted shirts over black pants. Their earlobes, elongated with beads, stretched to their shoulders. They looked like Masai tribesmen who had moved to the city to do business.

"*Jambo*," Katana said, greeting them in Swahili.

"Haallo!" the short man with pudding cheeks replied in African-accented English, smiling effusively. "I am Bond," he said, tapping his chest. "James Bond."

Despite her anxiety, Sabine smiled. Uncle would say James Bond had put on a lot of weight since they last saw him in the movie *Goldfinger*.

The warrior held the doorknob. His stern face was riddled with pain as if bitten by a tsetse fly. "We find missing people for a *fee*," he said, fixing a hardened gaze on them.

"I know. My uncle is missing." Sabine adjusted the shoulder strap of her handbag.

Eyeing the bag, the warrior nodded. "Ma'am, we find missing people every day. We are very thorough. We sandblast everything until ..." He paused.

"Until we find your loved ones, dead or alive," added Bond.

"My uncle's alive," said Sabine.

The two men exchanged glances. "As you wish," they said together. "Come in."

The office was sparsely furnished with a wicker sofa, a typewriter on the cowhide drum, and a pair of tiny triangular zebra-skinned stools. Katana sat on the floor, but Sabine called him to sit near her on the sofa.

The detectives perched on the zebra stools. The tall man's crane legs were stretched out like long arrows; Bond's stubby legs looked like short baseball bats.

Sabine had the feeling of being watched and looked around. Fierce masks on the side wall stared at her—faces of lions, wild rhinoceroses with grotesquely distorted horns, domed heads with concave eyes, faces with inverted lips and vertical ridges that ran from the forehead to the chin. The chalk-smeared eyes of the masks glowed like ghosts' eyes. Were these men witch doctors? Was she in the right place?

As if he'd read her mind, Bond opened a scrapbook and drew her attention to the photos of all the missing men they'd found. Sabine recognized a former minister, a journalist, and a priest. She had seen their pictures in the newspaper. Below the photos of the missing men, in red ink, were the dates they were found. She noticed that it took about a month to find them. Satisfied, she took a steadying breath and sat back.

The warrior cleared his throat. "Ma'am, we need the payment of our fees before we accept your case. We need to cover the costs of our investigation." He waved his pointer finger. "To find a junior official, our fee is five thousand shillings. To find an important person, twenty thousand."

"I'll pay *after* you find my uncle," said Sabine.

"*Alafu,*" Katana repeated in Swahili.

"English, please." The warrior's face turned as fierce as the masks on the wall.

"Ma'am, we give full guarantee or all your money back," said Bond.

"The fees, please," said the warrior, stretching his long arm toward Sabine.

Sabine reasoned. What was the worst that could

happen? They'd take the money and run. But if they did come through with any information at all, it would be worth its weight in gold.

"I can pay a deposit now." She emptied her purse, placing the bills of different denominations on the drum. "I promise to pay the rest later."

The thin hands of the warrior grabbed the money and stuffed it into a drawstring bag. He took a pen out from behind his ear.

"Name and address of your uncle?"

Sabine told them.

"Describe him."

Sabine took out the photograph from her handbag and gave it to them.

They looked at Uncle leaning against his sports car. "Ah! Zully, the safari driver," they exclaimed together.

"You know Uncle?"

"Who doesn't know Zully? He's the pride of Uganda," said Bond. "We cheered him at every Safari Car Rally."

Sabine leaned forward. "My uncle helped anybody and everybody in trouble." She told them about Uncle's car shop but withheld information about his passport business. She talked about how close she was to her uncle, how much she missed him.

Bond listened with a rapt expression, shaking his head in sympathy. He turned to his partner. "Isn't she like my niece?" And the warrior grunted.

They exchanged phone numbers, and Sabine stressed that she would call them.

Bond rose. "Ma'am, we need the blessings from the spirits of our ancestors to help us solve your uncle's case. Are you ready for the mask ceremony?"

Sabine nodded. She had been to a similar ritual during the harvest at the farm. Africans often called on the supernatural powers to assist them with their problems. Katana used to break an egg or step over sacred branches from the jungle.

Bond cleared the cowhide drum. He knelt on the floor and held the drum with one hand and strummed his other hand on it.

Dhum-dhum dhum-dhum dhum-dhum.

The warrior put on the mask of a wild rhino and strutted around the room, pelvis thrust forward. Then he jumped catlike in the air, emitting a strangled, throaty cry. The pitch of the drumbeats rose; they came faster and faster. The warrior shut his eyes and went into a deep trance, mumbling strange sounds. Then he bowed and kissed the floor.

He took off his mask and nodded at Sabine to indicate that their meeting was over. As she fumbled her way to the door after Katana, he followed her, saying in a stern voice, "Ma'am, make sure the balance of our fees is ready next time."

Sabine nodded, hoping fervently they would find Uncle quickly.

— The Raid —

October 11—16, 1972
DAYS 67—72

The war—if there ever was one—was over, but the curfew was still in effect. Every evening at the stroke of six, the lights in every house and every street were extinguished. And when night fell, the seven hills of Kampala were trapped under what seemed to Sabine like a big black burkha that wrapped them all in the dark while the countdown snared its prey.

Inside the house, Sabine and Mama made sure that candles glowed from brass holders in every room while Papa hung oil lamps on every doorway. The lamplight threw dizzying dark shapes and lurking shadows that danced on the walls.

Early in the week, Sabine got the opportunity to call the detectives.

"Ma'am, *vary* good you called," said Bond.

"You found my uncle?" Sabine's hand on the phone shook.

"Umm ..." He cleared his throat. "Ma'am, we think Mr. Zully ... ruffled a few feathers of some big birds at the SRB."

"The SRB?"

"The State Research Bureau, the President's special force."

The warrior came on the line. "Ma'am, we'll give you a full report soon. Remember to bring our fees when you come."

"Yes," said Sabine. City slickers they might be, but they seemed to be on the right track. She could hardly wait for the day when they gave her more information on Uncle. Then it would be a good time for her to spill the story to her parents. Papa would be so proud of her. And Mama would be beyond happiness.

It was day seventy-two in the countdown. Sabine and her family ate supper in silence except for the clinking of forks against china plates. They no longer talked. There didn't seem to be any point. Always it was the same—no progress on Uncle's case, or that So-and-So was leaving the country, or crazy rumours about the President.

The light from the oil lamp that hung in the doorway of the dining room picked up glints of silver in Papa's dark hair, and Sabine wondered when the greying had begun. He looked tired. His furrowed forehead showed signs of stress. She felt sorry for him. A heaviness sank in—how their lives had changed. Her eyes met Papa's, and the lines in his face softened.

Crash! The window across from Sabine shattered. *Kondos!* she thought. The chicken curry in her stomach churned as if the chicken had come alive.

"Get down!" yelled Papa.

They dropped to the floor. Crouching there, her body quaking, Sabine could hear every ragged breath, every thundering heartbeat in her ears. Her mind replayed the encounter she and Uncle had had with Butabika.

Papa drew near and beckoned for her to follow him while Mama helped the grinning Munchkin, who seemed to think they were playing a game. They all crawled to the sitting room and hid behind the sofa. The air crackled with tension.

"Sadru! Sadru!" the intruders chanted. "Toka nje! Out!"

They knew Papa. They couldn't be kondos. She looked at Papa, his face white as bone. "Papa, you must hide."

"I'm not leaving!"

"Sadru." Mama nudged him. "It's *you* they want."

"Paradise Place," Sabine whispered in Papa's ear, pushing him gently, keeping her gaze on him as he crawled to the kitchen, tried the back door. Locked. He climbed over the countertop and jumped out the open window.

Bang! Bang! Every bang on the front door felt like a gunshot to Sabine's chest. *Go away, please ... go away.*

Mama rose. "I'll see what they want. You stay here." But Sabine could not let her mother deal with the thugs alone. She caught Munchkin's hand and they followed Mama breathlessly to the foyer.

The door opened. Shadows advanced. The angle of light from the kerosene lamp magnified the shadows; they folded into each other like the multiple heads and limbs of a monster. The countdown that Sabine had heard on the radio every day had solidified into a creature and had arrived on her doorstep! She felt her heartbeat leave her body for a moment.

Two dark figures with guns barged into the sitting room, pushing a very scared Katana ahead of them. "We're from the army," one said, stating the obvious.

"I'll call the police," said Mama. Her forehead was shiny with sweat.

Mama is brave, thought Sabine. Just then a gigantic man pushed his way in front of the other two men and towered over everyone.

"We are above the police!" he bellowed.

He stood like a huge tree, his limbs as thick as branches. The massive form cast a malevolent presence like the ghostly baobab in Katana's stories. His half-buttoned military shirt was stretched over a heavily muscled chest. Fear paralyzed Sabine's chest and squashed her breath. Baobab's brute strength could squeeze the life out of them in seconds.

"Where is Sadru?" Baobab asked Katana, who just shook his head.

Baobab's fist smashed into Katana's face and sent him across the floor. Sabine screamed. Munchkin screamed too. Blood trickled from Katana's nose onto his shirt. Mama bent over him and pressed his nose with her scarf to stop the bleeding.

Sabine cradled Munchkin, trembling as she looked up at the giant. "Katana needs a doctor," she said in a shaky voice.

Baobab laughed. "Eti! Afraid your boi won't live to wash your underwear?" He edged closer and tottered in a drunken state, almost tripping on her. "Where's Sadru?"

"Papa's on a business trip," she said, her mind reeling. "Aunty's looking after us." She pointed to Mama, who nodded at her and rose.

"Can I help you?" asked Mama.

Baobab advanced. Mama retreated.

"Ha-ha!" Baobab's eerie laugh shattered the stillness. "I don't hurt pretty women." He fished out a dog-eared photograph from his pocket. "Do you work for him?" He tapped at Papa's picture. An ivory ring crowned each of the fingers of his thick hand.

In the photo, Papa posed with Bapa, their hands over each other's shoulders. At the far corner of the photo Sabine saw the legs of a man in military uniform, a man who was presumably too tall for the photo.

Mama's fingers flexed and unflexed. "Mr. Sadru is on a business trip."

"Why do you want him?" Sabine blurted.

"Uganda does not want troublemakers who poke their brown noses in military matters." His fleshy forefinger ran across his throat, and he made a deep, strangling sound that drowned in a crashing sound from the kitchen behind.

The startled soldiers cocked their guns. Sabine realized that Munchkin had slipped away. "Wait, please, it's my brother!" She caught Mama's hand and they dashed to the kitchen with the soldiers at their heels.

Munchkin sat with Milo on the floor, sucking his fingers. A can of Mazola oil lay sideways on the floor, the oil still spilling out.

Baobab kicked the can. "Search this house."

Mama lifted Munchkin with his Milo. The men rampaged through the pantry while the butt of Baobab's gun knocked down soup cans, tomato cans, and Ideal milk cans. He threw aside the jars filled with basmati rice, lentils, and mung beans. One swipe and all the neatly labelled spice bottles fell, scattering sticks of cinnamon, cumin, and cloves everywhere.

"Why are you making this mess?" Mama asked.

"Eti! You're hoarding and my people are dying of hunger." The gun jabbed Mama's back. "Move!"

They returned to the sitting room. Two soldiers searched the room, but Sabine's eyes were on Baobab as his head tipped back to admire the chandelier hanging from the ceiling. The multitude of crystal drops in the chandelier caught the light from the oil lamp on the doorway and transformed it into a thousand blue fires. His gaze shifted to the gilt-framed paintings on the walls; then he stared at the television screen as if caught in a magical moment. "Soon I, too, will live like a king, and all this will be mine." He tapped his barrel chest.

Mine, mine, mine—the word whirled round and round like Munchkin's yo-yo in Sabine's mind.

In the dining room, the butt of Baobab's gun hit the bowl of chicken curry. It splattered on the floor. Sabine saw the blue willow dinner plates of half-finished food on the table. Four plates—had Baobab noticed the number? She faked a fall, pulling off the lacy white tablecloth with her. *Crash!* The plates and cutlery fell to the floor. Mama helped Sabine to her feet, squeezing her hand to acknowledge her clever idea.

"Move!" yelled Baobab. They passed the alcove on the far right. He peeped through the French doors of Papa's office, tried the handle, and found it locked. His lips curled into a triumphant smile. He sent the two soldiers upstairs and turned to Mama. "Open it or I'll break it down."

Mama found the keys and unlocked the office door.

Inside, the Makonde sculpture watched mutely as Baobab flung open the drawers of the rosewood desk to find pens, pencils, and stationery. Cursing, he flung open the Zanzibar curio chest and found the House of Manji biscuit tin.

"Aayyy! Biscutti," he exclaimed with glee. "I like biscutti."

Sabine exchanged a quick glance with Mama. He opened the tin and gulped the biscuits. He checked for more biscuits in the tin and yelped as he came upon the currency notes hidden below the paper separator.

"Ah! Very good!" Quickly he filled up his pockets with the bills. "For my children," he said with a grin.

Sabine stifled a smile. Papa's ploy had worked.

"Move," yelled Baobab. They went upstairs and met the two soldiers coming out of Mama's room. "*Afande*, nobody's here," they said.

Baobab grunted. "I'll see you downstairs in a few minutes."

He sat on her parents' four-poster bed, the spring creaking under the massive weight of his body. "Nice," he said. He checked the dresser and dabbed Mama's perfume on his jaw. "Very nice," he said. He grabbed the comb and ran it through his wiry hair, then checked himself in the mirror, grinning.

"Move," he yelled again.

They went past the corridor into Sabine's room. The snakeroot hands swept all the books in the bookshelf to the floor. Another push across her bureau and her Russian nesting dolls and the photo of Sabine with Zena and the coffee bush fell to the floor, its glass frame shattered.

Munchkin dropped his stuffed monkey. He bent to get it, but Baobab's gigantic boot distracted him, and he pulled at the undone laces instead.

Sabine cringed.

Baobab's boot stamped on the monkey and pinned it to the floor. Wheezing and panting, Munchkin pushed at the giant boot, expending all his energy to move it, but he failed. He began to cry. Mama scooped him up and comforted him.

Baobab smirked.

Sabine stretched her neck and drew herself up to her full height, looking up at the giant fiercely. "Sir, that's my brother's toy."

"Is that so?" Baobab picked up Milo carelessly by its leg. Then he pulled out a flip knife from his pocket and held it up for them to see. His thumb pushed a button. *Ping!* The blade sprang forth, long and shiny and sharp.

A numbing terror swept through Sabine. Mama held Munchkin tightly.

Baobab tested the sharpness of the blade on his thumbnail; his nostrils flared as satisfaction registered on his face. The knife swung at Milo's neck, and the head and torso fell separately to the floor.

Monster! Sabine's hands clenched. Munchkin's face contorted and his eyes rolled back. He hit his head on Mama's chest, screaming.

Sabine picked up Milo's head and body and looked squarely at the giant. "We are Ugandans. You are supposed to protect us."

Baobab waved his knife, and his eyes, red as raw meat, burned with intensity. Just then the two soldiers returned upstairs and looked at the knife in horror. "Sir, the Captain said not to harm them," one of them said.

Captain? The only captain Sabine knew was Captain Asafa.

Baobab grinned. He slipped the knife into his pocket and followed the two soldiers down the steps. Sabine heard the heavy bootsteps recede and felt their vibrations through the soles of her feet until they died with the slamming of the door.

"My babies." Mama held them tightly; tears ran down her face, mixing with theirs.

They went downstairs to Katana and stepped gingerly around the broken glass and the coloured spice mounds on the kitchen floor. It looked like a tornado had ripped through and blown everything apart. Katana's nose had stopped bleeding, but it was red and swollen. It hurt Sabine just to look at it.

"My magic help," he said, showing off his feather.

"You are brave and loyal." Sabine rubbed his arm. She

had heard that many servants during the Mau Mau uprising against the British turned against their employers. She brought some ice, which Mama applied to his nose.

Sabine quickly unlocked the back door and called for Papa in the darkness until she heard his approaching footsteps.

"Papa!" She ran into his arms and he hugged her, his hands as cold as ice.

She had never seen Papa so broken before. He was her brave father, who ran a business empire, who was influential, who always protected them. It pained her to see him stand amid the debris on the floor, his hair mussed up and flecked with grass bits, his pants flapping against his calves in the breeze from the open door.

"Is everyone okay?" Papa asked in a faint voice, looking at everybody, flinching when he saw Katana's battered nose. He patted his head. "Pole, I'm sorry."

He went to Mama and they embraced. "I should have listened to you. We should have left." He slumped over, resting his elbow on the countertop, and as if on cue, the half-open bottle of turmeric fell off the shelf, adding more colour to the mess on the floor.

"Papa." Sabine shook his arm. "They're looking for you. You must leave now."

"I will not leave you all in this lion's den." Papa's dark brows knitted into one.

"Sabine's right," said Mama, her anguish buried in her wringing hands. "You can stay with your sister in Nairobi for a few days."

Papa winced.

"Sadru, it's *you* they want," said Mama. "They had orders not to harm us. We'll be safer here than if we left together now." She added, "Bapa will come, keep an eye on the business. We'll let you know when it's safe to return, or else we will follow you."

Finally Papa gave in. He didn't have a choice. He would go by bus to Parin Aunty in Nairobi, as flying was risky if the soldiers were on the lookout for him. Mzee would drop Papa off at the bus station in Mama's car. Sabine found his passport in his office while Mama dumped a few toiletries into a bag for him.

Hugs and kisses were hastily exchanged. "My brave boy," Sabine heard Papa whisper, and she managed not to cry. "Look after your brother and mother." One prickly brush on her cheek, and he left. Gone.

The night stretched into a hundred and one nights. Katana slept on the sofa downstairs. Mama called Bapa at his farm and told him briefly about the raid, and he said he'd come at once. Mama also called the police, but Sabine knew it would not help. The army ruled.

Sabine slept on her parents' big bed next to Mama and Munchkin and his taped-up Milo. She pulled at the satin bedspread; it appeared to still hold the contours of Baobab's body, which sent shudders up her backbone. How would they survive without Papa? She snuggled closer to Mama as she did when she was young. Papa had left her in charge as the man of the house. She would protect her family and, with the detectives' help, would find Uncle.

— Mama —

Sabine woke up with a start on her parents' big bed. Munchkin lay curled up, snoring in his sleep, next to his wounded Milo. Then it all came back: the raid and Papa's escape.

Downstairs, sunshine illuminated the kitchen and the marble floor sparkled. It smelled of soap and Dettol. Katana must have cleaned up all the evidence of the raid. Sabine saw her mother, bony elbows propped on the table, holding her head in her hands. Instinctively she knew something was wrong. "Mama, are you all right?"

Mama looked up. The enlarged whites of her eyes matched her white salwaar kameez.

Sabine's skin prickled. "What happened? Did Papa call?"

"Papa is fine," said Mama, breathing heavily, her shoulders rising and falling, sagging a bit lower with each breath. She held Sabine's arm for a moment, then let it go.

"Sit, dear."

Sabine remained standing. Blood pumped through her head as she desperately searched her mother's face for clues.

"Commissioner Karanja called. Papa's stuck at the

border town of Tororo," said Mama. "Immigration officials in Kenya refused to give him a visitor's visa. They don't want Indian refugees."

Sabine shuddered involuntarily. Nobody wanted them. If only Uncle were here. One phone call to the immigration officials and the problem would have been solved. "What will we do?"

Mama leaned forward and her voice dropped to a whisper. "They want chai." She rubbed her thumb against her forefinger to indicate money.

"Then let's give it to them." Sabine didn't care if bribing was wrong. Sometimes wrong could be righted only by wrong. Besides, Uncle had always said it was the only way for Indians in Africa to get things past the government officials.

"We can arrange to send the money to them," said Mama. "But ..."

"We can't trust them. They can take the money and run."

Mama nodded. "We can't wait for Bapa, either. He may get there too late for Papa."

Bapa had left in his lorry for Kampala, but the farm was an eight-hour drive west of Kampala. Tororo was in the other direction—six hours east of Kampala.

Sabine's index finger scraped at her thumbnail helplessly.

"I don't mind going to Tororo," Mama said softly.

"You?" Sabine looked at her mother, surprised. Mama, soft and tender as her pashmina shawl, always worried about Uncle and Papa and their safety. Wasn't she afraid for herself?

Mama regarded Sabine intently for a disconcerting moment as if evaluating her decision. "My concern is you and Minaz," she said. "I can't leave you alone."

"We're not alone. Katana's here. Bapa will soon be here. We are fine, Mama."

Mama twisted the ends of her dupatta. "The soldiers came after Papa because he probed Zully's case. He did it for me. It's my fault."

"It's not, Mama, but it doesn't matter," said Sabine. "What matters is that you must leave now or it'll be too late for Papa." She caught her mother's arm. "Don't worry, Mama, I'll look after Munchkin."

Mama inhaled deeply, considering everything, then nodded. She would ride in the Akamba bus for six hours to the border town of Tororo. She rose. "I'll ask Lalita to stay here until Bapa arrives."

Sabine did not want Lalita, but she did not want to argue.

Sabine sat at the kitchen counter, dragging a spoon through her porridge, making small circles inside big circles.

"Jambo," said Katana, padding into the kitchen in his flip-flops, a yellow duster on his shoulder.

"Jambo," she replied, flinching at the sight of his nose. The swelling had subsided, but now there was a dark purple discolouration. It pained her to see the bruise and she turned her gaze away. "Does it hurt?"

He shook his head.

"Come, sit. Some chai will make you feel better."

He smiled, showing all his teeth, and reached out for his plastic mug on the top shelf.

"No, Katana." She picked up one of the the willow-patterned china cups they used regularly. It was time to make some changes. She and her family had been treating the Africans like the untouchables in India. Katana could not share their utensils, could not use their washroom. As if he'd pollute them. Every day he waited until they finished their meal; then he cleared the table, washed the dishes, and sat on the kitchen floor to eat the leftovers or to cook the bubbling white *ugali,* a corn mush. Sabine's face felt hot with shame. It was not only Mr. Singh or Lalita who were prejudiced, but she and her family as well. The whites and the soldiers, too. They were all prejudiced.

She poured tea into the china cup, feeling good. "Here," she said, offering the cup to Katana.

He seemed confused at first. He looked over his shoulder cautiously, then accepted the cup. He added three heaping tablespoonfuls of sugar to his tea and stirred it and looked around again. Satisfied, he sat on Papa's chair. Despite his shortness, he sat straight and tall, as Papa did. He held the handle carefully and touched his tongue to the lip of the cup. Then he looked up and gave Sabine a shy, appreciative smile.

"Ah! *Mzuri sana,* vaaary good. This be my best chai."

Mama and Munchkin returned, bringing Lalita with her toxic aroma of lavender. Lalita beckoned Sabine toward her and kissed her noisily on both cheeks. Sabine wiped off the lipstick marks with the heel of her hand and sank on the armchair in the sitting room.

Lalita cast her sharp eyes to confirm that Katana was not within earshot; then she leaned forward. "Guli-bhen, be careful when you phone home."

Mama frowned. "What do you mean?"

"The line may be tapped." Lalita's kohl-lined eyes smoldered. "You don't want the dogs to catch Sadru-bha."

Recognizing that Lalita had a valid point, Sabine said, "Mama, we can talk in food code. If things are fine, mention sweet food like ladoo. If not, mention karela." It was such a bitter vegetable that she could not imagine how anybody could stomach it.

Mama nodded. The two ladies looked at Sabine and beamed.

"Yes, and in case of danger say red-hot chilies," added Lalita, taking charge as if it had been her ingenious idea all along.

Mama rose. "I'll be back in two days, and then we'll all leave together."

Sabine nodded, hoping the detectives would find Uncle by then. She did not want to leave without Uncle.

Lalita amused Munchkin while Mama packed, pausing frequently to glance anxiously at Sabine.

Impulsively, Sabine threw her arms around her mother. "Don't worry. We'll be fine."

Mama's arms came back around her into a warm, rose-scented hug. "Sabine dear, I am proud of you."

That was precisely what Sabine wanted to tell her mother. Papa was the head of their family, but Mama was the heart. But when she looked into Mama's eyes, the words were trapped in Sabine's mouth, and what came out was, "Oh, Mama!"

Mama in her white salwaar kameez and dupatta around her shoulders looked like an angel with wings. What ... what if she didn't return?

A sob gathered in Sabine's throat. Long ago, she had made fun of her mother for being a worrywart. Now *she* was the one who worried. She shifted her gaze to the ceiling, blinked, and swallowed a lump of despair.

"Sabine," Lalita called, tilting her head toward Munchkin and rolling her eyes to signal a warning.

Sabine nodded. One last glance at Mama and then she led Munchkin away. "C'mon, let's play," she told her brother, and he thrust his colouring book at her. "Okay, then, let's colour," she said, and led him to the dining table.

They began to colour. Sabine felt utterly lost and alone. Uncle had left her, then Zena, then Papa, and now Mama. Both of her parents said she was brave, but she felt anything but that.

What was courage, anyhow? Maybe there were different kinds of it. She looked at the crayons in the box. Yellow for Uncle's courage—he brought sunshine to everyone's life. Blue for Papa's nerves of steel. White for Mama, angelic in her love and care. Green for Bapa, who conquered the land. What of herself? What colour was she?

Soon Munchkin pushed his colouring book aside. His woeful eyes panned the house for Mama. Sabine was worried that he would throw a temper tantrum, but thankfully Lalita came to the rescue. "I'm your mother for a few days, okay?" She lifted Munchkin and began to dance with him, singing his favourite nursery rhyme.

Later she cooked some alu gobi curry and called Sabine over to eat, but she politely declined. Lalita insisted. "Eat a little, so Mithoo eats too, na."

Sabine ate, reluctantly at first. It was delicious. She was surprised at herself when she took a second helping. Lalita, sitting across from her, smiled smugly. They watched television for a while, and then Lalita took Munchkin to bed.

Sabine waited for Bapa. She looked at the night sky through the gaping hole of the dining room window. It was still and silent outside except for a stir of living things in the undergrowth. She gazed at the Milky Way arching brightly to the horizon. Uncle, who had travelled all over the world, had told her that he had never seen such bright stars as the ones here. She thought back on all the wonderful times she had with Uncle and Zena.

Now the sky, black as death, appeared to be riddled with a thousand bullet holes. Sabine envisioned the countdown monster lurking in the darkness. Its treelike limbs had ivory-clawed tentacles. Its piercing military eyes burned with vengeance, and on its left cheek were three scars.

She shuddered, drawing her mother's shawl tightly around her shoulders. She had lived here all her life, yet she felt she was a stranger.

"It's an illusion." She repeated it like a mantra. She would not sleep in her room alone. She would wait here until Bapa came. She sat on the sofa.

Bina, it's always darkest right before dawn. Uncle's voice.

Sabine was not alone. She would not give up.

— Bapa —

October 18, 1972
DAY 74

Sabine awoke to the tantalizing scent of cinnamon. She had fallen asleep on the sofa while waiting for Bapa. She took in a deep breath. Her stomach growled. She loved cinnamon. Zena had baked a cinnamon cake for her last birthday.

Sabine found Bapa at the kitchen table in his usual khaki safari suit. He was chatting with Katana, who was washing dishes at the sink.

"Bapa!" She ran to him.

Bapa smoothed her hair and rained kisses on her forehead. She could smell the red earth of Kasenda and the aroma of coffee beans. She held his big, dry hand, not wanting to let go, as if she were holding on to the fun times she'd had with him and Zena at the farm.

"Bapa, when did you come?" She looked at his crinkled eyes, the colour of rich Bugisu coffee. It matched his sun-soaked skin.

"Late at night. I didn't want to disturb your sleep."

He took her forearm and finger-wrote on it the letter *S* for Sabine, laughing as he always did. She laughed as well, though there was certainly little to laugh about.

"Beta, you've grown!"

"You, too," she said. She began to count the crinkles

on his face, one crinkle for every year of his life. "One, two, three ... seventy-five, Bapa."

"Ho! I'm getting younger. Didn't you count a hundred last time?" He prodded her to sit down and poured some milk for her. "Katana has baked cinnamon cake for you."

"And for Minazi and Bapa," added Katana, beaming.

Sabine thanked Katana and helped herself to the soft cake, relishing the sticky sweetness of the cinnamon as it dissolved in her mouth. "Mmm ... so good!"

"Eat, eat." Bapa put another slice of cake on her plate. He poured the tea from the cup into the saucer, held it with both hands, and slurped.

Munchkin stumbled into the room in his blue-striped pajamas holding on to Milo and crying. He ran from room to room as if frantically searching for something he had lost. He was looking for Mama. Sabine and Bapa went after him and found him slumped in a corner of the foyer. Bapa carried him to the kitchen and tried to coax him to eat, but he pushed his plate away.

Soon Munchkin became Sabine's shadow, tagging after her wherever she went. He banged on the door if she went to the toilet. She tried to colour with him, but he whimpered. She brought his toy cars and lined them up on the floor and called him to play car crash. But he sucked his thumb, making slurpy sounds like a newborn kitten lapping milk. If only he'd cry, scream, anything, she'd know he was fine. Finally, a hint of a smile spread on his face when she made his favourite drink of Milo. She made him sit on her lap the way Mama used to, and helped him drink it.

That day, after the countdown on the radio, a song played.

Mgeni siku ya kwanza	Guests on the first day
Mpe mchele na panza	Give them rice with coconut
Mgeni siku ya pili	Guests on day two
Mpe jembe	Give them a hoe
Mgeni siku mingi	Guests of many days
Mpe mteke na migumi.	Give them a kick and a fist.

Bapa said that the song was adapted from a Swahili poem for guests.

"But we aren't guests," retorted Sabine. "I'm fed up with all this."

"The laws are for the expatriates. Don't worry, Beta— soon you'll be in Kasenda, where the birds and streams sing, where the sky is bluest, and there are no soldiers, no guns, no laws."

Sabine didn't respond.

"You want to see Cheetah and Kasuku, yes?"

She still didn't respond. Kasenda would not be Kasenda without Zena and Ssekore. Finally she said, "Bapa, why do the soldiers come up with something new every day?"

"Beta, after the coffee's planted, it faces droughts, floods, pests. We must tough it out, yes?" He smiled.

She nodded, though she felt differently.

"Got to face the storm if we want the fruit, yes? Only a patient man will get to eat ripe fruits."

She was tired of Bapa's farming laws. Some of them were unjust. Why did some crops get good weather and others drought and disease? She wanted to believe Bapa, but she didn't. His wisdom seemed empty, as empty as the space inside her.

"I don't want any fruit," she blurted. "It's rotten."

All she wanted was for things to return to what they were before the stupid dream of Dada Amin's messed up their lives.

Bapa played with Munchkin while Sabine waited anxiously for Mama's call. She looked back and forth between the clock on the wall and the phone. If she stared at the phone intently enough, maybe she could will it to ring.

At last she heard the most pleasing sound ever. Her hand trembled as she raised the receiver to her ear.

"Sabine, how are you?"

Mama's voice seemed to come from a million miles away, but her warmth made Sabine's eyes blurry. She mumbled a reply as best she could.

"Lalita's brother is eating ladoo and gives you his love," Mama said.

Sabine felt a delicious jolt. Papa was safe!

Mama said she would return home the next day. Sabine handed the phone to Bapa and broke into a dance.

I will dance, dance, dance. She flung her arms out and danced to the sweet music that played in her ears. She danced, her heart turning cartwheels of excitement, her wild, tangled hair bouncing on her shoulders, as she sang a prayer of thanks to all the gods. She pulled Bapa and Munchkin in as well, and soon they were all dancing. At last, good things were coming Sabine's way. The storm had abated for now.

— The Warehouse —

October 18, 1972

DAY 74

When Bapa took Munchkin out for a walk in the park, Sabine called the detectives. She hoped they had made a breakthrough in Uncle's case. What a great surprise it would be for Mama when she came home.

"Ma'am, we got vaaary good news," said Bond.

Sabine's heart lurched. She could not wish for anything better. "Did you find my uncle? Did you?"

"A few muhindis from the prison have been transferred to the warehouse. Mr. Zulfiqar could be one of them."

Strange, thought Sabine. Why were the prisoners held in a warehouse? They must have no room in the prison, she decided.

"Can you find out if my uncle is there?"

"Ma'am, we need our fees before we proceed."

She had to be cautious. "I'm sorry I can't pay until I get some results."

"Ma'am, we work at supersonic speed. Right now, we're on our way to the warehouse, but we need our fees."

"Then I'm coming with you."

"No, no. The warehouse is not suitable for a young lady."

Did he think he'd dissuade her? "Do you want your fees?"

"Hold, please hold."

After a long pause, the warrior came on the line. "Ma'am, finding people is vaaary expensive. We need the next installment *before* we proceed," he said firmly.

"Eight hundred shillings and *I'm coming*," she said in an even firmer voice. "I'll pay the rest later." Thank God, Mama had left some money in case of an emergency. They agreed to meet outside the office.

Sabine called for Katana, but there was no response. Hastily she scribbled a note for Bapa. She'd tell him everything after she returned. She took the money and slipped it into an envelope for the detectives. Ah! She then put a lollipop into her pocket and rushed out into the hot sun to look for Mzee.

In the car, Sabine imagined her union with Uncle.

"Uncle, where were you lost?" she'd say.

"I missed you, Bina," he'd say, drawing close till their foreheads knocked.

She'd show him the lollipop, and he'd chuckle and tease her by saying, "I missed them more than I missed you."

She would punch him playfully and refuse to give him the lollipop.

The pair of detectives sat on the hood of their blue pickup like a pair of jackals, in dark glasses and shiny black faux-leather jackets. Sabine waved to them, and they jumped off the car and ran to her car window.

She handed the envelope to Bond.

"Thank you, ma'am." Bond grinned broadly, his teeth

sparkling like the white keys of the harmonium that Uncle often played at music parties.

The warrior took the envelope from Bond and counted the bills inside, a thick copper bracelet wound around his wrist. He looked up and smiled at Sabine, his very first smile, and stowed the envelope in the inside pocket of his jacket.

Satisfied, they set off. Mzee tailed the detectives' blue pickup closely as they passed the Kasubi tombs, the final resting place of the Baganda kings. On top of the hill was the former palace of the Kabaka of Baganda, who had once ruled Uganda. Soon the road gave way to a rutted, uneven terrain, and the pickup's engine stalled and conked out.

Sabine watched anxiously as the moments ticked away. Bond hopped out of the pickup and lifted the hood. He put a straggly bit of wire into his mouth to stretch it and then fitted the wire someplace inside the engine and waved to the warrior to start the car. Miraculously, it gurgled to life. Bond closed the hood and returned to the pickup and they hit the road once more.

They stopped at a tumbledown building that slouched like a sick old man bent over in pain. Cracked plaster had peeled off the walls, exposing the raw red bricks underneath, and the dried wood pillar supporting the canopy looked like the old man's walking stick. A line of crows perched on the broken roof tiles. Sabine could barely read the faded sign: UGANDA MEAT WAREHOUSE.

"I'll be back soon," she told Mzee, getting out of the car before he could object.

She followed the detectives' rustling footsteps through tall elephant grass that reached her knees. The yellow dandelion heads peeking out of the grass field shone like stars in the sun. She swallowed. Zena had accused her of being a child of dandelions. She plucked a sunny blossom. It may be a weed, but it's pretty, she thought defiantly, and pinned it in her hair.

They stopped at a clearing. The warrior stood storklike on one leg, leaning on the shaft of his tribal spear. "Ma'am, first we have to drive out the *chen*," he said.

"To satisfy the spirits of the dead," added Bond.

Sabine nodded.

The warrior checked his bearings, mumbled an incantation, aimed, and threw his spear. It flew in a high arc over the grass field toward the west. Bond explained that when the sun set, it would carry all the evil away with it. Now, with the spirits appeased, they made their way to the dilapidated warehouse. The warrior took long, loping strides, followed by the stumbling Bond, and Sabine halfrunning to catch up.

Suddenly the crows on the roof flapped away in a frenzy. The marabou stork had landed. The huge, ugly bird clacked its sharp bill, drawn out like a butcher's cleaver.

Sabine cringed. The marabou was like a vulture: it ate the dead.

The warrior flung stones at the marabou, and its wings fluttered as it challenged them with a shrill scream. Bond burst out laughing, his belly wobbling.

Sabine ran ahead of them into the sanctuary of the

warehouse. An unpleasant odour assailed her in the dimly lit reception room. Two unshaven guards sat on straight-back wooden chairs playing cards, their heads rocking to the African song from a tiny transistor radio. Above their heads, a single lightbulb dangled precariously at the end of a long frayed wire, crusted and blackened with fly excrement. Flies buzzed over half-filled soda bottles next to an open logbook on the old wooden table.

The guards looked past the detectives and stared at Sabine with curiosity.

"Jambo," Bond said, greeting the guards. "We're looking for Mr. Zulfiqar."

The guards exchanged glances and resumed playing.

Bond nudged his partner's elbow. The warrior dug into his pocket and brought out a folded bill and Uncle's photo, the one Sabine had given them earlier.

"Rafiki, friend," said the warrior, pressing the folded bill into the hand of the guard, "we're looking for this man." He held out Uncle's photo.

The guard leapt to his feet and clicked his heels. He looked at the photo and exclaimed, "Ah! Muhindi! Check room three." He pulled open a drawer and took out a key and a flashlight. "You'll need this."

"Thanks, friend," Bond said, and accepted the items.

Sabine followed the detectives down the wooden steps through the dark, cavernous interior into the bowels of the sick old building. Ahead, it seemed the walls were coming closer together, squeezing out the air, but she fought off her claustrophobia. She had to find Uncle.

Bond pointed the flashlight for her. "Ma'am, see you don't fall."

The beam made strange-shaped silhouettes on the walls. Except for the squeaks and cheeps of their footsteps on the wooden steps, it was deadly quiet as they groped the unsteady banister along the musty passage.

They stopped at a closed door. Bond rammed his shoulder against the door to open it. "Nobody here," he said, shining the flashlight around the room.

Sabine ran into a cobweb hanging limply in the corner like a fishnet. "Yuck!" She shook her arm to get rid of the sticky bits.

"Sorry, ma'am." Bond flicked the strands off her arm and wiped his hand on his pants. "Don't worry. There won't be any creepy-crawlies in the freezer room."

Did they hold prisoners in cold rooms to torture them?

The flashlight shone at a door and Bond yelped, "Room three, ma'am." He tried the rusty iron handle. It was locked. He brought out the key the guard had given him and fitted it into the lock. He turned the key, and with a soft click the door unlocked.

Sabine quivered in anticipation as Bond held the door open for her. A cold draft rushed out as she stepped inside. Hot air from outside collided with the cold air inside and made a mist that hung in strange, ghostly shapes. She felt the dampness of the mist on her skin and shivered.

The warrior's beam flashed and Sabine saw rows of dangling plastic bags hanging vertically on giant meat hooks attached to rollers. She looked up. The rollers were suspended on steel rods attached to the ceiling like the curtain rod in her bathroom.

Inside the plastic bags were ... bodies. Human bodies.

She stared. The horror tore at her eyes. She had seen carcasses of cows and goats hung by their legs on metal hooks at Bismillah Butchery when she went with Mama. Abdulla, the butcher, would cut the meat, trim the fat, weigh and wrap the meat for them. A strangled cry caught in her throat. She convulsed. They couldn't, couldn't ... *couldn't* be. But they were. Dead. Dead. Dead.

Her mind raced. This is a dream, she told herself frantically, a nightmare. Her eyes closed, and when she opened them she saw the bodies again. A virulent stench lodged in her sinuses, and she held her breath as long as she could.

The detectives read the brown nametag taped to each body bag, and fragments of their conversation drifted over to Sabine.

"African ..., no name ..., African ..., African ...," said Bond.

"African..., Singapore treatment ..."

Sabine saw crisscross scabs on the arms and legs of the corpses. They had been tortured. Terror seized her. She gasped, reeling backward.

"The cuts are neat ... cut right through the joints ..."

A sickness swept over her. She groaned. She was not going to make it. She took out her handkerchief and coughed into it.

The detectives checked a pile of body bags stacked carelessly on the floor like firewood. "Storage problem," said Bond. "The dumping lorry is late."

Sabine recalled Katana's talk of the "river treatment" and the "sledgehammer treatment," and ghostly specters from the body bags appeared to rise and hover here, there, everywhere. She gripped Uncle's model car and his lollipop in her pocket as she steadied herself and found her voice. "Where are the live prisoners? Where's my uncle?"

"Wait, I find muhindi," Bond cried in an excited voice of discovery.

Oh, no. Sabine caught her lower lip between her teeth and said a silent prayer as she waited for them to read the nametag.

"No name," said Bond.

Sabine wheeled around, heels poised to run. "Let's get out of here. Now!"

"As you wish, ma'am," said the detectives together.

Bond pointed the flashlight beam and Sabine made her way cautiously along the dank, dark passage, up the spiral steps, back to the reception area.

"No luck," said Bond, returning the key and flashlight to the guards, still playing cards.

"Check the old records." One of the guards pointed, without raising his head, to a red plastic bucket in the corner heaped with brown tags.

The detectives walked toward it, but Sabine stopped them. "No, my uncle's alive. I have to talk to you." The detectives trailed after her as she left the building.

Outside, she turned to face them. "I hired you to find my uncle," she said firmly. "Why did you bring me here?"

"Ma'am, you insisted on coming," said the warrior.

"The warehouse is temporary storage for dead prisoners," said Bond. "We came to check the bodies before they are emptied into the lake. Otherwise, how will we know if Mr. Zulfiqar was here or not?"

"I thought you were *detectives*. You are supposed to find missing people."

"We are bodyfinders. Dead or alive, we find your loved ones," said the warrior.

"Understand, ma'am, please," said Bond. "We take the short route for your benefit. To save you time and money, we work baaackward from Z to A."

"Work forward then. My uncle's alive," she said.

"We'll work whichever way ma'am wants," said the warrior, digging his little finger into his ear.

"I won't pay any more fees until you find my uncle."

"As you wish," they chanted together.

"Missy, missy." It was Mzee. He had followed them inside. Sabine ran to him. He held out his arm and helped her to the car, mumbling reproaches at himself. This was not a proper place for a young Indian girl to visit.

They pulled away from the warehouse or mortuary or whatever it was, but the stench of death stayed with Sabine, lodged into her nostrils. Her head banged, her heart banged, and her stomach banged. The countdown hidden in the cavernous abdomen of Uganda was multiplying, spreading evil cells, invading everything—colour, tribe, religion, and occupation. All she could do was cling to hope beyond reason.

— New Rule —

October 18, 1972

DAY 74

Katana opened the door and hollered, "Bapa, Bapa, Sabine be back."

Bapa shuffled to the door, his forehead cracked into a hundred fissures. "Beta, where did you go?"

Sabine leapt into Bapa's arms and burrowed in his warmth. Munchkin tried to push her away, wanting Bapa for himself. Bapa pulled him into the embrace as well and then led them inside.

As they sat on the sofa, the dreaded words squeezed out of Sabine's throat in jerky bits. "The detectives investigating Uncle ... the bodies hanging from meat hooks ... the warehouse." She shook her head, trying to shake off the stench of death. "Bapa, it was horrible! You can't imagine!"

Bapa's face shrank.

She talked and talked, paying no heed to Munchkin as he poked a finger into her forearm. It was only when Munchkin got up on the sofa and began to pull her hair that she finally stopped. Katana carried Munchkin across the room to watch television.

Bapa's hand fell on Sabine's knee, and she felt his tremor. "Beta, you've been very brave, but I would die if anything happened to you," he said. "I will deal with the detectives myself. You must promise me not to contact them again."

She nodded. "Bapa, we must report the killings!"

He shook his head. "They'll silence us and continue what they are doing."

"Don't worry, Sabine," said Katana. "The spirit of dead will take revenge."

"We can't wait for the dead," she said. A wave of helplessness washed over her as she realized that the law of the gun would prevail. Fate had tied their hands and muffled their voices. Bapa nestled her head on his shoulder, and she tried to numb her feelings by watching the adventures of Tarzan on the television.

But the program was interrupted. Suddenly they were looking at President Idi Amin at a military parade at City Square. Huge and imposing, like Baobab the giant, the President filled up the screen, his uniform crowded with badges and medals that he had mostly awarded to himself, inventing titles and achievements. Smiling effusively, he held up his hand like the Queen of England, and the audience chanted, "Dada, Dada, Dada!"

A pressure built inside Sabine. Every cheer for the President raised her anger another notch. They were rooting for him as if he was a superhero, when in fact he was responsible for terror, torture, and the deaths of hundreds. Perhaps thousands.

Munchkin began to march too, swinging his scrawny arms in a soldierly way.

Sabine exploded. "Stop it!" she said, but he ignored her.

On TV the newscaster began a long announcement. "Indians who claim to be Ugandan citizens must take their documents to the Immigration Office for verification. Those who got their citizenship through corruption or forgery will be rejected. *Kipande*, identification cards, will be issued to legal Ugandan Indians next week from Monday to Friday. They must carry these cards with them at all times."

A new rule! Sabine looked at Bapa. "We were born here," she said indignantly.

"They want to do a census for the Indians. A mere formality."

"Bapa, it's like when Hitler ruled Germany, and the Jews were forced to identify themselves by wearing the Star of David." She had read *The Diary of Anne Frank*.

Bapa hunched on one side heavily, as if his other side had given up support. "Beta, we have to do whatever needs to be done. Thousands are affected. I'll call Commissioner Karanja, see if he can help get our documents verified so we don't have to stand in line for the cards."

Sabine lost steam. Bapa was right. She nodded, breathing out short, sharp gasps. Once again she thought of Uncle. If only Uncle were here—he would have gotten the cards for them in no time. Uncle knew all the immigration officials.

She played with Munchkin, her ears on the alert for the doorbell to ring and for Mama's footsteps. Instead, the phone rang.

She grabbed the receiver. "Hello …"

It was Mama. "We eat ladoo every day, but we miss you and Minaz."

"Us too, Mama," Sabine replied in a fake cheery voice, eagerly waiting to hear when her mother was coming back.

"I have a problem, dear. I can't return, not without that new card, the kipande."

Sabine's jaw dropped. The new rule. "Mama, if you give Bapa the passport particulars, we'll get the cards and mail them to you." She gave the phone to Bapa and fled upstairs so she wouldn't dissolve into tears.

Clutching her mother's amber beads, she prayed fervently in English, Gujarati, Swahili, and Arabic. Surely one of the gods would understand her. Halfway through, the Swahili saying on Zena's gown that Sabine had worn when they danced flashed into her mind.

Dua la kuku halimpati mwewe. A chicken's prayer will not keep away the hawk.

"Well, mine is a lion's prayer," she said fiercely aloud. "I am Simba's child. A lion can scare a hawk away."

— Kipande Line —

October 27, 1972
DAY 83

The early morning sun, a mild turmeric-coloured blob, chased the crescent moon from the sky as Sabine trailed behind Lalita and Munchkin along Parliament Avenue, flanked by red canna blossoms. Her satchel, filled with documents and other necessities, weighed heavily on her shoulder. Bapa had tried all week to get the kipande cards so they would not have to line up, but failed. So he flew to Fort Portal, his town of residence, to get his card while Lalita accompanied Munchkin and Sabine to get theirs.

The traffic congestion forced Mzee to park on the street across from the new City Council building, where he'd wait. Lalita rustled along in a dusky rosebud sari holding Munchkin's hand, singing his favourite Gujarati rhyme, *A, B, C, pot with ghee* ... Sabine, although grateful to the queen for coming, was embarrassed by her loudness. She slowed down.

Lalita waited for Sabine to catch up, then pointed to the offices of the British High Commission, farther away. "That's where I have to go for my visa."

Sabine acknowledged Lalita with a nod and a smile. The British government had done away with its quota system and was now issuing visas by the hundreds to all Indians with British passports.

Ahead, the kipande line coiled and curved for hundreds of yards along Jinja Road, a long, bright slithering serpent whose head was the tall, red-brick Immigration Office building. Its jaws were the double glass doors that opened every few minutes to let a few people in and then closed.

The waiting Indian women wore saris and salwaar kameez in bright popsicle hues. Some of them sat cross-legged on the grass, looking like flowers that were growing there. Their husbands stood in dark suits at their sides, emotions hidden behind dark glasses. Only the children smiled. So many communities: Punjabi, Hindu, Bohra, Ithnashri, Sikh, Ismaili, and Goan. They had only one thing in common—their skin colour. Brown.

Sabine joined the end of the line and became the tail of the serpent. Katana's song played in her mind. *Shamu the serpent, sleek and supple, slender and sly, as long as night, slowly, slowly, oh so slowly, swallowed its own tail.*

"Ar're, what nonsense are these Africans up to," said Lalita. "If we stand in the sun all day we'll turn black like them."

"Then we won't need the card," Sabine joked. She knew that under Lalita's shell of racism lay a well of kindness. "Aunty, I'm glad you came."

"Thank Ram I'm not Ugandan!" Lalita snapped.

Sabine gulped. What a twist of fate! Her own family, who were Ugandan citizens, were trapped with nowhere to go, while British Indians like Lalita, who didn't trust Africans, could just go to Britain. And then there were indigenous Africans like Katana, who were scared to death, and those like Mzee, Zena, and Ssekore, who were anticipating the best of times. It all depended on the hand fate had dealt.

Lalita spread her rosebud shawl on the grass, and they sat on it. Sabine saw a few familiar faces in the line—her classmates, Mama's friends, Pirbhai Uncle and his family. They must have camped all night to get their prized spots in the front, she concluded.

Lalita played with Munchkin. "I spy blue," she'd say, and Munchkin would touch a few things. "Na, na." She'd shake her head and her earrings would dance. If he touched a blue object by coincidence, she would clap and he'd squeal in delight.

"Today is day eighty-three. One week remains for Indians to leave Uganda."

The countdown was stalking Sabine. She glanced behind. A young lady in a lehnga with her dupatta draped around her head sat by her old father on a reed mat, their ears glued to a tiny transistor radio. Sabine swallowed as she recalled the day Zena had worn her lehnga. How beautiful she had looked.

Pesky flies and mosquitoes darted in and out while peddlers sold sodas, salted groundnuts in newspaper cones, and ice cream from the Lyons Maid van. Every few minutes Sabine shifted and strained to check the progress of the line. Too slow. Her head ached and her neck was stiff as a board. It would take forever.

Her eyes felt heavy. Not having slept the last few nights, she drew up her knees and put her head on them. She thought of the blue waves lapping and dreamt that she and Uncle were fishing and they caught a huge fish, which they pulled and pulled ... until Lalita's sharp voice interrupted.

"*Sala nakama!*" Lalita spat, looking in the direction of the soldiers.

Sabine saw the soldiers lounging on beach chairs under plantain trees. Usually Indians and British bwanas sat inside offices while African servants toiled in the sun. Tyranny had turned Uganda upside down and back to front. She'd tolerate everything if only Zena were her friend again and if only she found Uncle.

"They hate us," Lalita said with venom.

"Aunty, our superior attitude distances us from them. They do not understand us. They hate us because they feel threatened by us."

Lalita's finely arched brows shot up. She didn't say anything.

The sun climbed the sky until it reached its peak at noon, when, sleek and gold, it glowed with pride. Sweat streamed down Sabine's face and her eyes hurt. She had not brought her sunglasses. She rubbed her knuckles into her eyes. There was nothing she could do. Her mouth was dry, even though she had been drinking constantly. Thankfully, Munchkin amused himself, scuffing his feet, raising clouds of red dust.

A mosquito buzzed near Sabine. She slapped at it, but

it flew away. The pesky bug returned and sat on her arm, waiting—just like the soldiers—to extract her blood. She let the pest flicker on her arm for a while, then slapped again. This time she squished the blood sucker.

She glanced behind and took comfort in the fact that hundreds more had joined the kipande line, which meant that they were now in the belly of the serpent. A baby cried and the mother undid the blouse of her sari to breast-feed. As Sabine turned, she caught sight of Lalita swaying.

"Aunty!"

She grabbed Lalita's shoulders to steady her, then lowered her until her head rested in Sabine's lap. "Aunty, what's wrong?" She touched Lalita's red forehead. It was hot. She squeezed water from the bottle in her satchel onto her hanky and dabbed it on Lalita's forehead.

The young lady behind them fanned a newspaper at Lalita's head. "Heat stroke," she told Sabine.

Soon Lalita sat up. "I'm fine," she said, but her face was still flushed.

"Aunty, you are sick. You must go home with Mzee," Sabine insisted.

The proud and defiant Lalita refused at first, but soon she was forced to give in. Before she left, she fired warnings at Sabine in a weak voice. "Don't leave the line ... don't lose any documents ... don't look at the soldiers." Lalita handed a stainless-steel tiffin lunchbox to Sabine and walked slowly away, a kind man helping to steady her.

"Ahhhh!" Munchkin pulled on Sabine's hand, wanting to go as well.

"I have something nice for you," said Sabine. She opened the tiffin and they ate Lalita's delicious samosas.

The afternoon heat intensified. Hot air seared Sabine's lungs and let loose rivulets of sweat down the back of her neck, under her arms, under her knees, and down her calves. She was glad Lalita had left. The heat fed the waiting Indians with languor, but it seemed to feed the soldiers with energy: they began to take frequent rounds of inspection. She played with Munchkin, sketching funny faces in the dirt with a twig, keeping her head low, as Lalita had warned her plenty. She could try to hide from the soldiers, but not from the heat that engulfed her like a furnace.

The young lady behind them poured tea from her thermos flask for her old father. Barely had he raised his cup to his cracked lips when a soldier yelled, "Mzee, come here!"

The old man rose slowly, supported by his daughter's arm. He hobbled with laborious breaths, the cup shaking in his wrinkled hand.

The soldier grabbed the cup, flung the tea on the grass, and threw the cup.

The old man sank back onto the grass, sobbing, "What wrong did I do?"

Sabine was enraged. If only she had a rifle, she'd ...

Munchkin whined. "Are you tired?" She took out Milo from her satchel and gave it to him. She cradled his head on her lap, chasing the flies over his head until he dozed off. As the line crawled forward, she dragged the sleepy Munchkin along.

When he woke up, he began to scream. "Eeeeee!"

Sabine knew he needed to pee, but she had heard there was a huge line to use the toilets at the American Embassy on Parliament Avenue. She counted—twenty families in line already. She hesitated.

"Take him there." The young lady pointed to a tree. "I'll keep your spot."

"Thank you," Sabine said with a grateful smile. She took Munchkin under the tree, where a strong urine odour wafted. She felt dirty and ashamed.

On their way back to their place in line, they ran into Pirbhai Uncle with his family. Aunty was crying unashamedly. "We can't stay, can't stay. They said our papers were forged."

Questions shot out at them: "Where will you go? What will you do?"

"Become refugees, what else?" said Pirbhai Uncle.

Sabine was worried. She had only two passports in her satchel and photocopies of her parents' passports. Would the army officers accept the photocopies?

Soon only one family was ahead of them. She waved to the ice cream man in the van. She bought a choco-stick for Munchkin and put Milo away in her satchel. The ice cream would keep him occupied while the officer verified their documents. Her stomach was all fluttery; she would buy ice cream for herself later, on their way back.

At last she heard the word she had waited all day to hear. "You," the soldier said, waving his baton at them, and they stepped through the glass doors into the coolness of the building.

— Verification of Documents —

A stern bespectacled clerk led Sabine and Munchkin down the corridor, past several rooms with Indian families. At the end of the corridor, the clerk knocked on the door, opened it, and left.

Inside, the windowless room was like a smoke-filled tomb. Clouds of smoke hid the officer's face. Sabine checked on Munchkin and wiped his chin where some of the chocolate from the ice cream had dribbled.

"Papers."

The voice. It resonated in Sabine's ears. Her hand shook, but she managed to pull out the folder from her satchel. The smoke lifted a little, and she saw two giant feet in shiny black shoes, laces undone, propped on the wooden desk next to a brown bottle of *waragi*, a local liquor fermented from bananas that was often advertised on the television.

She placed the documents gingerly on the desk.

The giant feet disappeared from the desk. A pair of thick hands grabbed the documents. An ivory ring crowned each finger. Sabine's breath died with her realization of who he was. Those snakeroot hands could belong only to the soldier who had raided their house in search of Papa. Milo's executioner. Baobab.

She turned into a sack of rattling bones. *Breathe,* she told herself. *Breathe. Act normal.* Eyes down so he wouldn't recognize her. Thank God, Milo was inside her satchel.

"How many in your family?"

"Four," she stammered. Phew! He didn't know her.

"Born?"

"Here, I mean Kampala," she said. Couldn't he read the documents?

He crossed his thick, treelike arms behind his head and reclined. "Go to school?"

"Yes, sir," she said. Why did he ask useless questions when hundreds were scalding in the hot sun? *I'll say yes-yes to everything, take the kipande cards and scram.* She glanced at Munchkin. He was busy licking the last of his ice cream.

"Very good." He reached for a blue card, stapled her photograph to it, stamped it, and gave it to her.

Sabine dropped the card into her satchel, relieved. That was easy.

He leafed through the other documents and looked up. His eyes, red as raw meat, bored into her. "Where are your parents?"

Sabine scratched her arm. "Working," she said.

"Eti! You Shahs, Sharmas, Patels are 'paper citizens.' You sit and make money while my brothers walk for hours in the sun to lead the cattle to pasture."

Sabine's hands at her sides balled into fists as she struggled to keep her rage contained. Her nails dug into her palms. Papa worked hard—that was why he made money. When a pigeon-pea shrub has no flowers, it blames the sun.

"These papers are useless." He crumpled the photocopied documents into a ball and flung it into the wastebasket. "I need the originals."

Sabine's fists clenched so tight that she felt her bones would snap. She glanced at Munchkin. His fingers dug into his nostrils. He did that when he was uneasy. She drew him near her. "What about my brother, sir?"

Red eyes scrutinized Munchkin, blinked, and refocused, the vitreous gleam caught as if in an *Aha!* moment of awakening. "We need no idiots," he said.

Sabine was on fire. "He's not an idiot," she said indignantly, wishing she could burn this man to cinders. "He's my brother."

"Ha-ha!" The laugh of triumphant victory. "Eti, Sadru ran away like a scared rabbit."

Sabine's whole body convulsed. He knew who they were.

"Don't be afraid. I don't hurt pretty girls."

Sabine stared at the stack of blue kipande cards on the desk, an arm's length away. She could easily grab the cards and run. Desperate people take desperate measures. No, that was a criminal act. She was no criminal. She recalled that he liked their house. "Sir, my father can build you a house like ours."

He sprang to his gigantic height. "I'm going to get your house anyhow, but right now the warmth of a pretty girl like you will make me happy."

He pushed his face so close to her that she could see the network of red capillaries on the whites of his eyes. Oh!

She wished she could shrink, disappear, die. She wedged her satchel in front of her as a shield.

"You Indian chocolates, why do you keep to yourselves?"

Ogre! Get him, get him! a voice inside Sabine screamed. She wanted to grab the waragi bottle on his desk and smash it in his face. She glanced at the door and her eyes measured the steps. Nine.

"You understand?" He looked at her, into her, holding her with his lewd eyes.

Sabine wrenched uncontrollably as his snakeroot hands touched her cheek. "Don't!" She pushed him away. "Keep your dirty hands to yourself."

"Eti, dirty because I'm black!" He grabbed Munchkin's passport and ripped it up.

"My brother's passport!"

He threw the pieces in the air like confetti. "If you behave, I will fix everything for your family." He came closer to her again.

Pthoo!

Her spit glob hit his eye and set him off balance. One dark hand caught the wall, and the other flew up to wipe his eye. He looked as if he could not believe what she had done.

Neither could she. She grabbed Munchkin's hand and they ran down the corridor, out of the double glass doors, out of the jaws of the serpent.

— The Run —

October 27, 1972
DAY 83

Run, run, a voice inside Sabine urged as she tugged Munchkin's arm sweeping past the blur of faces in the kip-ande line. She heard someone call her name, but she kept running.

"Can you see Mzee?" she asked Munchkin, glancing at the hundreds of cars parked by the City Council building. She could not linger here. It was dangerous to be in the vicinity of the immigration building. She dragged Munchkin along and ran down Jinja Road.

A stitch knifed her right side, but she kept running, her breath whistling as air rushed in and out of her lungs and sweat ran down her face. She wiped her face on her sleeve and swung back for a quick glance. Thank God, no one was chasing them.

"Ahhhh!" Munchkin pulled against her.

She slowed down. On the shoulders of Kampala Road they blended into a swarming crowd of shoppers bustling to catch the bus and hawkers shrieking bargain prices over unsold fruits and vegetables at the end of the day.

They passed the crowded bus depot. It looked like a good spot to hide and rest. They sank down onto a concrete retaining wall behind an out-of-service bus, breathing heavily, while the idling buses exhaled belching black fumes.

"Good boy!" She patted Munchkin's back. "Now we're far from that bad man, okay?" She felt a strange mix of joy and disgrace. Strong and good to have avenged the disgusting soldier, yet ashamed of her spit attack.

They must go home. Bapa would be waiting for them. She turned to Munchkin.

"You want a ride on that double-decker bus?" She pointed. "Let's take Milo home."

Munchkin smiled.

She caught his hand and led him into the thick crowd of impatient people waiting to catch buses at the bus stop. They fell into the line of people waiting to board a bus to Nakasero and were carried forward by the flow of passengers behind them.

Inside the bus, everybody stared at them. All of them were Africans. All the seats were occupied, and passengers jammed the aisle with baskets of fruits and vegetables and protruding stalks of green plantains. Munchkin's nose wrinkled. The bus reeked of a cocktail of odours—diesel fumes, sweat, and ripened fruits.

The conductor pushed his way through the aisle. Sabine paid the fare, and he printed the tickets from a machine hanging around his neck and pressed the tickets into her hand, shoving and ramming her into other passengers as he did so. "Move, move, always room for one more."

They squeezed themselves toward the back of the bus until they stood near the exit door, their backs pressing against the backs of other passengers.

The bus rumbled away. Sabine held tight to the steel rack at the top while Munchkin clung to her. At each bus stop, the driver started up again even while passengers were getting on. At the lights, the driver slammed on the brakes so hard that Sabine and the rest of the standing passengers fell on each other like a pack of cards.

"Ouch!" cried Sabine. Someone had stepped on her foot. She wondered how Zena and Ssekore could stand riding the bus regularly. Finally, as more passengers disembarked, she got a seat next to an African man and pulled Munchkin onto her lap.

The man looked at Sabine and smiled. "*India jai che?* Going to India?"

Sabine shook her head and returned his smile. He must have picked up Gujarati while working as a servant for an Indian family. The man asked that her family give their house to him when they left or else the soldiers would grab it for themselves. She nodded and smiled politely.

The bus climbed Nakasero Hill, and she breathed easier in the familiar surroundings.

When Sabine reached home, her sweat-drenched dress was plastered to her legs, her socks and shoes sopping wet. She crumpled into Bapa's arms and clung to him, not wanting to move. Never before had she been so afraid.

Bapa held her close and pulled Munchkin in as well. "Beta, where's Mzee? Why didn't he bring you? How did you get here?"

"Bus, we came by bus," she said, bursting to tell all, but Munchkin began to cry.

Bapa led them inside, his arms around both of them. Sabine opened her satchel and gave Milo to Munchkin. Bapa put Munchkin's head on his lap on the sofa, patting him, and he dozed off.

Bapa put his hand on Sabine's arm and rubbed it while she told him about the kipande line. She squeezed his hand as the horror of Baobab's advance came back to her. A shiver went through her, and Bapa's hand tightened on hers. She told him how Baobab ripped up Munchkin's passport and of her spit attack and the bus ride.

Bapa blew air through his pursed lips. He shook his head sorrowfully. "Beta, it's not safe for you to be home. We'll move into a hotel tonight and leave for Kasenda tomorrow. I'll inform Lalita." He rose to phone her.

I am a fugitive. A sense of shame permeated Sabine. She felt humiliated at having to escape like a criminal. Well, she'd done what she had to do.

If they left for the hotel, Katana and Mzee would be worried when they came to work the next day. Hastily she scribbled a note for them and put it on the table under the crystal bowl of pomegranates, when she caught sight of a brown tag.

Hadn't she seen that at the ... the ...?

She picked up the tag with trepidation. A chill raked her flesh. The nametags were taped to the body bags at the warehouse. There had been a plastic bucket of tags too.

Uncle's name, Zulfiqar Manji, was on the tag. Beside

it was the date, August 25. A week after Uncle had disappeared.

"Bapa!" she screamed. Her stomach tightened up like her fists. "Where did this come from?"

Bapa put down the phone and rushed to hug her.

"Who gave this to you?"

Bapa's face crinkled like crunched old parchment paper. He nodded without saying anything, then nodded again. "I was going to tell you, but ... but ..." His scratchy voice broke and his head collapsed into his wrinkled hands.

She pulled at his hands, wanting to see his face. "Bapa, tell me," she said, though already the brown tag had told her everything.

Bapa's misty eyes struggled as he tried to contain his grief. He looked down at his palms as if studying the creases and calluses.

"I ... I met the detectives. They found this tag and traced it to the logbook of records at the warehouse." He looked up. "I'm sorry, Beta. I didn't want to tell you when so many bad things have happened to you."

Sabine gasped and folded into herself. Pain pulsed in every part of her body, but she had no tears left to cry. She stood immobile, staring at the ripe pomegranate in the crystal bowl. It split open in her mind, the redness spilling ...

"Bapa." She clung to him, her heart wrenched.

"So sorry, so sorry," Bapa kept saying.

She looked again at the tag in her wet hands, staring

at Uncle's name, wishing, praying, that the blurred letters would change, desperately hoping it was a mistake.

But she knew it was not.

Uncle was dead. She had suspected it for some time, really; otherwise Uncle would have called. Her suspicions grew when she saw the dead bodies at the warehouse, yet she had prayed for a miracle. Now the tiny seeds of hope in her were crushed. She closed her eyes, praying that Uncle had not suffered.

Bapa said Lalita was coming to the hotel with them and reminded Sabine that they had to leave right away. "Beta, pack a few things while I get some clothes for Minaz."

Sabine nodded. Baobab might come to the house for her. There was no time to grieve.

Sabine scanned her room. She had to pack her life's belongings in a few minutes. What would she take?

She found Uncle's model car under her pillow and slipped it into her pocket. Uncle was with her, inside her. She would keep him alive by cherishing her memories with him. The soldiers couldn't take him from her. *I will not let them win.*

What else should she take?

She looked wistfully past the collection of books to her bureau, picked up the cracked photograph of herself and Zena in front of the coffee bush. Would she ever see Zena again? She dropped the photograph into her duffel bag.

Her hand closed on her silver anklet with bells. Every day she had strapped it around her feet and danced. She and Zena had whirled and twirled like spinning tops, dancing their joys. She dropped the anklet in her bag as well. The bells tinkled eerily in the hush.

Her room overflowed with stories of her life. Stories she could not pack in a bag. Her legs felt weak. She sank onto her bed. She smoothed her satin bedspread and straightened the pillows. Who would sleep in her bed? Who would own her beloved books? Who would wear her clothes? How could she just leave?

Meow. A lone cat outside whined like a wounded child. A shiver tore through Sabine. Fear hung like a cold noose around her neck. She caught her reflection in the mirror and was startled to see her stricken features. *I am not a quitter.*

She must hurry. The sooner she left home, the safer she'd feel. Hastily she grabbed a few clothes and some toiletries, stuffed them into her bag, and dashed out. The hinges groaned as she closed the door behind her.

Outside, a chilly wind bristled through the mango trees in their backyard, bending the black branches of Paradise Place, to wave to her.

"Goodbye," she whispered. "I will miss you."

She looked at their house. It's just a house, she thought. It became a home only when it was filled with the love, trust, and hopes of her family. Turtles carry their homes with them so they are always at home. *I will carry my home with me.*

"Goodbye," she whispered again.

— The Sky Be Very Angry —

October 27–28, 1972
DAYS 83—84

Silence reigned inside the car and outside in the dark deep night as Bapa drove them to the hotel. Lalita sat in the back seat, one hand on Munchkin sleeping on her lap, the other tapping Sabine's back gently to ease her grief. The moon and the stars were tucked in the bed of black clouds, grieving too, or perhaps hiding in shame. The streets were deserted even though the curfew had been lifted. Kampala looked like a ghost city.

Bapa slowed down, and Sabine heard a loud breath whoosh out of Lalita's mouth like a doomsday sigh. She looked out the window. Lurking under the shadow of the streetlight, among other parked cars on Kampala Road, was a military jeep. So many thoughts rushed through her mind: she would scream, she would run, no, she would trip the soldier, grab his rifle, and ...

Luckily, no one stopped them and Bapa sailed past without a problem.

Lalita found her voice. "O Ram! Ram!" She thanked her god over and over. "Better to eat dry roti than stay here in fear, I tell you."

They pulled up in front of the Apollo Hotel. Named after the *Apollo 11* space mission, it was the most prestigious hotel in Uganda. A uniformed bellboy came out to help them, and Bapa opened the trunk of the car to let the bellboy unload the luggage.

Lalita held Sabine's hand while Bapa half-dragged and half-carried the sleepy Munchkin inside. At the doorway red and green Christmas lights flashed on and off, and over to the side stood a big Christmas tree decked out in tinsel and ornaments. From the top of the tree an angel figurine looked down at Sabine with tenderness.

The hotel lobby bustled with Indian families chatting over chai. The familiar sight of saris and salwaar kameez, the lyrical sounds of the Hindi and Gujarati languages, and the tinkling of bangles took Sabine back to Little India. They were all in the same boat.

Bapa put Munchkin on the leather sofa and went to check in at the front desk. A few ladies chatted with Lalita. Sabine heard them say that Indian families had flooded the hotels in the city as the soldiers were ransacking big, isolated homes. Many Indians at the Apollo were British emigrés like Lalita; others had split families, with a few members approved and others rejected, their documents confiscated or torn up like Munchkin's. Sabine also heard stories like hers, of women being harassed by army officers.

She took the keys from Bapa and headed to the room. She and Lalita were going to share a room, and Bapa and Munchkin would share another.

She called Mama and told her about their move to the hotel. "Mama, we can't get the cards. You can't come here. We'll help Lalita get her papers and join you in Nairobi soon. Then when the storm's over we'll try and return home."

Then she told Mama about Uncle.

"God bless," said Mama softly, followed by a few seconds of silence. Mama seemed to have accepted the news calmly, as if she had been expecting it.

Sabine talked to Lalita late into the night. She had suspected that the soldiers had killed Uncle, she told Lalita, but it was easier for her to pretend that he was alive. While she had held on to the illusion, her mother had accepted Uncle's death and moved on.

The next day Bapa took Lalita to the British High Commission to get her visa. Sabine was alone in the hotel room when the front-desk clerk called.

"A Mr. Katana is here to see Miss Sabine."

Sabine's heart skipped a few beats. "I'll be down in a minute," she said. Excited, she did not wait for the elevator and ran down five flights of stairs to the lobby.

The bellboy held Katana by the shoulder, near the Christmas tree at the entrance, releasing him only when he saw Sabine.

"Sabine!" Katana ran to her in his lime-green flip-flops.

In the luxurious surroundings of the hotel, he looked totally out of place wearing Papa's oversized blue shirt over khaki shorts with his sleeves rolled up to his elbows. "I read your note, so I come." He added, "Mzee sends *habari*, greetings."

Sabine thanked him.

"You forgot Mama Guli's jewels," he said, thrusting a bundle tied in a pink lace-edged handkerchief into her hand.

"Thank you," she said again. She untied the bundle and found the diamond brooch that Mama had kept for her. "For your little Sabine," she said, giving it to Katana.

"Asante," he said, bowing once, bowing again.

She saw her set of gold bangles. "Can you please give this to Mzee for his granddaughters."

Katana nodded and slipped the bangles and the brooch into his pocket. "Any news of Bwana and Mama Guli?"

"They are doing well. I will join them soon."

Sabine looked at his animated face and chewed on the soft inside of her cheek. When would she see him again? *Would* she see him? It hurt her to leave him in the claws of danger, for the soldiers were hunting the Langis. All she could do was to pray for him—that is, if God was listening. Often, she felt, God was hard of hearing.

"Goodbye, Katana!" she managed to say.

"Please take me with you," he pleaded, wiping a tear.

Sabine wished she could. For years he had looked after her, cleaned up after her, told her stories and songs to coax her to finish her meals. "I will take your stories and your songs, okay?"

He nodded, but he looked disappointed. His lips moved silently as he struggled to say something. Nothing.

"If you come with me, then how will you visit your wife and your little Sabine?"

"But you, Minazi, Bwana, and Mama Guli be my family too."

An avalanche of emotions tumbled inside Sabine. She choked as she tried to hold back the tears that welled up in her eyes. After a moment's silence, she found her voice. "We'll return as soon as things get better."

"Okay," he said, forcing a smile.

She drew closer to hug him, but he took her hand and kissed it instead, saying, "Go, go to a nice safe place 'cause the sky here be very angry."

She nodded, turning her wet face away from him.

"Don't cry, Sabine," he urged. "I send you fresh matoke and brown eggs from my *shamba*." He began to sing, "*Mungu, O Mungu, bless her who is Simba's child. Bless her who's mightier than the hyena. Bless her journey, far away.*" He stepped back slowly toward the exit door, not letting her out of his sight.

She waved at him, smiling through her tears, until he finally turned and left.

Lalita returned to the room, smiling from ear to ear, waving her visa like a flag of victory, her gold bangles tinkling.

"Ar're, Little India is black. Every shop on Allidina Visram Street is run by golas, blacks. Curry Pot's still closed. No one can run my teahouse," she said with pride.

Sabine asked who had taken over Uncle's car shop, but Lalita didn't know.

Lalita prattled on. "I went to buy a shirt for Mithoo. I ask the price of an Arrow shirt, but the new owner, a soldier, shrugs. Then, ah! He looks at the size label on the shirt and says, 'Size fifteen, oh, give me fifteen shillings. Size fourteen, oh, give me fourteen shillings.'" She giggled.

"Aunty, it is our fault. We took advantage of them, didn't pay them well, didn't give them time off, didn't allow them to learn skills—"

"Better they face us than Santa Amin," snapped Lalita. "Ar're, let me show you my present to myself." She slipped her hand inside her sari blouse and brought out a ticket. "It's flexible so I can turn in the unused portion in England for refund in sterling pounds," she squealed.

Sabine smiled. Lalita was shrewd. A new departure law placed a limit on the amount of savings they could take with them, so Lalita had spent her "useless" Ugandan currency to buy a round-the-world ticket.

Lalita stowed the ticket back in her blouse for safe-keeping, pulled her sari tightly across her chest, and looked at Sabine. "Your turn, Sab. Tell me what you did."

Sabine related Katana's visit.

"He's a good African." Lalita opened her purse and pulled out a pair of gold earrings. "I'll tell Hasham Bapa to give this to Katana's little Sabine."

"That's very nice of you." Sabine hugged Lalita.

It would have been a good day if only Baobab had not crashed into Sabine's dreams that night and stolen her sleep. She stared at the ticking hands of her watch for a long time, careful not to shift in the bed and awaken Lalita. All Sabine wanted now was to get out of this hellhole as soon as possible.

— High Tea —

October 29, 1972

DAY 85

Sabine and Lalita met Bapa and Munchkin for high tea, a tradition from colonial days that was maintained by all the upscale hotels in Uganda. The sunny garden in the courtyard of the Apollo brimmed with flowers, and soft English music serenaded from the speakers hidden amid the shrubbery. In the centre of the courtyard, water gushed from a stone sculpture of the crested crane, the national bird of Uganda. The crane stood on one leg to symbolize that the country was moving forward. How ironic, Sabine thought, but she didn't say anything.

They sat on wrought-iron chairs around the fountain, drinking tea under the shade of multicoloured umbrellas. African waiters in white uniforms and red fez caps with tassels wheeled trolleys covered with cream cakes, pastries, and pies. Sabine didn't know what to choose, but Munchkin cooed and filled his plate.

They drank the tea and admired the flowers around them. In Kasenda, Sabine and Zena used to collect the jasmines from Bapa's garden and steep them overnight in water, and the next day they would dab the jasmine perfume behind their ears.

Bapa showed Sabine the flamboyant gold mohur,

the porcelain rose, and the bird-of-paradise. He said the Ugandan soil was so rich that these flowers grew like weeds.

Soon Munchkin became a nuisance. Probably he'd had too much sugar. He dipped a finger in her cake and licked it, smacking his lips, and when she scolded him, he swung his leg and kicked her on the shin. Thankfully, Lalita took him to the bathroom.

The music on the radio gave way to the countdown. The noose around Sabine's neck was tightening. She didn't care. The monster had only a few days of life left.

"Today is day eighty-five. Five days remain for all Indians to leave Uganda. Those who do not leave will be sitting on fire, and they will not be sitting comfortably."

The rule targeted *all* Indians.

Sabine looked at Bapa. "Bapa, we can't stay here!"

Bapa frowned. He seemed to be deep in thought.

She looked at the flustered Indians around them. An agitated Indian man in a suit yelled obscenities in Swahili. A woman pushed her cup of tea off the table. Sabine caught a wry smile on the face of the African waiter who cleaned up the mess.

She turned back to Bapa. "Bapa, what will we do? Where will we go?"

"Beta, there is no need to go anywhere. Sadru and Guli can come here later."

"Bapa, we can't stay here."

Bapa's age-spotted hand caught the back of her chair for support. "I can't leave. I mean ... I won't."

"Bapa, they'll kill you."

They stared at each other.

Bapa scooped a fist of red soil from a flowerpot. He opened his palm to show Sabine. "Beta, the Kasenda earth is soaked with my blood, my sweat, and my tears. My farms, the coffee beans, they're part of who I am. This is home. Halima and I cannot leave our home."

Sabine frowned. "Bapa, the rule does not apply to Halima."

A stormy look came across Bapa's face. His shoulders sagged and his head hung low as if a very heavy weight pressed upon him. For the first time she saw her grandfather crumple in front of her.

He cleared his throat. "Halima is ... special," he said with tenderness.

Special? Sabine's throat closed. What was so special about his farm manager?

"Halima and I live together." He looked down at his feet, his toes poking out of his leather sandals, curling and uncurling.

"You mean—she's your ..."

Bapa nodded.

Sabine broke into a sweat. Nobody had told her that. She recalled the photograph of Bapa and Halima in Papa's office.

"Sadru and Guli didn't approve of me marrying an African," he said, letting go of the soil in his hand.

"I'm so sorry, Bapa!" Sabine's heart wrung. Bapa was tangled between the world of Africans and Indians just as she was with Zena and Ssekore. Poor Bapa had lived a life of shame, silence, and secrecy because her own parents were as prejudiced as other Indians. She threw her arms around him. "I love you, Bapa."

"I love you, too." He kissed her on the forehead. "Beta, I was lonely after your grandmother died." His eyes turned into twin brown pools of pain. "Halima helped me grow new roots. She gave me hope, strength, and purpose in life."

She squeezed his arm. "Bapa, I will always love you, no matter what. I like Aunty Halima," she said. "But Bapa, her brother, Captain Asafa, raided our home to kill Papa!" she blurted, giving voice to her suspicions.

Bapa shook his head. "No, no, no. Asafa saved Sadru. Asafa's regiment was issued with orders to kill Sadru after he insisted that the army probe Zully's case. Asafa sent his men to the house to scare Sadru into leaving. What Asafa doesn't know is that one of his men is a rotten mango."

"Oh!" Sabine recalled that the soldiers who raided their home warned Baobab not to harm them. Indeed, the Captain was brave to swim against the tide of his men's hatred of Indians. "You mean Captain Asafa put himself at risk to save Papa?"

Bapa nodded. "Asafa adores Zena and knew how close she was with you."

Sabine bit her tongue. All along she had blamed the Captain. Truth was blurry.

"Beta, you and I have kipande cards. I can hide Minaz and ..."

"No, Bapa." She broke away from him. African waiters were clearing the tables. Overhead, the sun painted the evening sky with soft shades of pastels: pink, orange, and indigo. Fireflies flashed neon-blue lights, and the crickets chirped. Sunset in Uganda was surreal. She felt trapped in this beautiful land. How could she leave Bapa alone? What would she do without him? What should she do?

She picked up a fallen swordlike pod under the gold mohur plant and split it open. Her palm closed on the dry black seeds. *Go, go, go. Yes, no, yes, no. Go, go, go. Yes, no, yes, no.* She couldn't stay here, and yet she didn't want to leave.

The image of the Makonde sculpture in Papa's office glowed in her mind. Papa had entrusted her with the responsibility for their family. Without Bapa, how would she glue the broken pieces back together to make one happy family again? The seeds in her palm fell through the gaps between her fingers, one by one. A breeze stirred and carried the seeds away.

She would have to let go.

A plan grew in her mind. Bapa and Halima would stay in Uganda, but she and Munchkin and their parents would leave as refugees. It would be hard to live in a new place without Bapa, without Zena, without Uncle, but they would manage.

Sabine had heard that refugees were accepted in Europe, the United States, and Canada. She had drawn maps of these places in her geography class. But how would they live in a place they had never even seen?

I am Papa's brave boy. No. I am his girl, his brave girl.

—

Sabine phoned her mother and explained to her that the
expulsion law now applied to all Indians, citizens or not.
And that since their whole family was leaving Uganda, it
was safe for her to speak to Papa.

Papa's booming voice came leaping over the line, and
Sabine's heart soared. He comforted her about Uncle's
death and said that he longed to see her and Minaz.

She told her father of her plan. "Papa, I'm going to
apply for refugee status for all of us, but Bapa will stay with
Aunty Halima in Kasenda."

Papa agreed, but with obvious hesitation. "Sabine,
you have everything under your belt. I'm so proud of my
brave—"

"Girl," she quickly filled in. "Papa, I'm your girl."

After a moment's silence, he said, "Of course. You are
my brave girl."

— A New Sabine —

October 31–November 1, 1972
DAYS 87—88

Sabine held Munchkin's hand and followed Bapa into a tall glass building in downtown Kampala. She had come to apply for refugee status for her family. The United Nations had set up a temporary office to deal with Indian refugees. Bapa told her that there had been eighty thousand Indians in Uganda. Some had left already, but there were still thousands who needed a place to go.

The entrance to the office tower was crowded. Bapa held on to Sabine and Munchkin as they wedged their way through the wall of people. Much to Sabine's surprise, the people were kind and helpful. As she pressed on, a lot of them moved out of her way, even though there really was nowhere to go.

Once more she stood in a line of anxious Indians waiting to get into an office, but unlike the kipande serpent, this line was shorter, swifter, and friendlier, and there were no soldiers. She saw that all the people coming out of the office had relieved faces. Their hands gripped forms of one colour or another.

Bapa chatted with the man in front of him. Sabine overheard that Indians were being sent to refugee camps scattered in different parts of the world. Some families were split—father in England, mother in France, some siblings in Portugal, others in America. Sabine didn't want her family split apart. What would happen to them?

In a while, her number was called and they were ushered inside the office. A lady official with kind blue eyes attended to them. Sabine related her encounter with Baobab and how he had torn up Munchkin's passport.

The lady gave Sabine some forms, which she filled out with Bapa's help. The forms needed photos. Bapa smiled. "No need to line up for them," he said, and brought out photographs of Sabine and Munchkin from his wallet. Sabine saw that he kept Aunty Halima's photo there as well. He stuck the photos on the completed forms and handed them to the lady, who left the room. Sabine closed her eyes and awaited her fate.

Soon the lady official came back, smiling. "Congratulations," she said. She shook Sabine's hand and gave her the refugee papers stamped by the United Nations officials. "Canada welcomes you and your family." She gave Sabine the forms and two free airline tickets and wished her *bon voyage*.

Sabine stared at the tickets. One more day—then she and Munchkin would fly to Nairobi and continue their journey with their parents to Canada. She burst out crying, not knowing why. Bapa gave her his handkerchief, and she dried her tears. Once she was able to talk again, she smiled, thanked the lady and hugged her, and then hugged Bapa and Munchkin.

Back in the hotel, she found her satchel and ran to the

courtyard with it. She took out her kipande. "My turn!" she said aloud to the sky, to the birds, and to the world, and she ripped the card to pieces. *Rip, rip, rip.* It felt good.

She threw the pieces over her shoulders to the west, the way the detectives had thrown their spear, so that when the sun set, it would carry all the evil away.

The next day, however, fear returned. Sabine heard from others at the hotel during breakfast that the road to Entebbe Airport was lined with military checkpoints. Fresh terror seized her. What if Baobab was on the lookout for her?

Back in the room, she watched Lalita on the floor, struggling to fit everything in her tin trunk. "Ar're, what to take, what to leave?" fretted Lalita. A new departure law restricted them to twenty kilograms of personal belongings and one hundred dollars in foreign currency.

Suddenly Lalita giggled. She grabbed a pair of scissors, cut the pillowcase into thin white strips, and wrapped them as a bandage on her forearm over her stack of gold bangles. "No one will bother an old lady with a broken arm, huh?"

Sabine smiled. Nobody could beat Lalita for shrewdness. No wonder the Africans hated Indians like her.

The scissors. A different idea uncurled in Sabine's mind. She picked up the scissors and extended them to the surprised Lalita. "Aunty, I need your help,"

Lalita regarded Sabine for a moment, then slapped her forehead. "Ah! I see." She giggled, accepting the scissors. "Are you sure?"

"Yes, Aunty," said Sabine. She spread newspapers on

the carpet and pulled a chair up to the mirrored dresser. She removed her hairclip; a cascade of curls fell to her chin. "Aunty, I'm ready."

Lalita draped a towel over Sabine's shoulders. *Snip, snap, snip, snap.* She tested the scissors a few times and then began to cut across Sabine's thick tresses.

Black curls fell on the newspapers.

"My, my, look at you."

Sabine looked in the mirror to see a strange boy staring at her. She spun back, only to realize that she had seen her own reflection. She looked in the mirror again and saw her newly exposed earlobes. She ran her hand over her head. Her new short hair, sharp and resilient, sprang back. Well, if she hadn't recognized herself, Baobab wouldn't either. She did look funny. Uncle would have laughed. *My Bina's turned into Prince Charming.*

Lalita was pleased. "You look like my sweet-sweet Mithoo."

They met Bapa and Munchkin for supper. Munchkin poked a finger into Sabine's arm, showing no reaction to her short hair, but Bapa's snowy brows bunched into an arch and he laughed, the same conch-shell laughter as Papa. She missed Papa. He too would have laughed if he were there.

"Beta, you look cute. I want a haircut, too!"

"Sorry, I don't cut white hair!" Lalita joked, and they all laughed.

It felt good to laugh. Sabine could hardly remember the last time something had seemed so funny.

They ate in silence. When they made their way to their rooms, Sabine stopped midway in the corridor. "Bapa, what will we do without you?" she asked.

He squeezed her hand. "Beta, kismet brought me from India to Africa and I made my home here."

Sabine smiled. "Now kismet will take me to the new world and I will make my home there." It was her turn to squeeze Bapa's hand.

— Searched to the Skin —

The day had come. Sabine's last day in Uganda. It was hard for her to believe that she was leaving. She checked the tickets again. Departure 6:00 p.m. Seven hours away. She felt a strange mix of excitement and sadness. She longed to be with her parents. Tomorrow, the countdown would die.

"My sweet-sweet girl," Lalita said, cradling Sabine's face in a motherly gesture. "Aunty's going to miss you. You must promise to write to me every week."

Sabine nodded. Lalita was leaving for London on the same day. Her departure time was after theirs, and Sabine was glad about that.

She put on one of Bapa's shirts and made sure it hid the tiny peaks on her chest. She ran the brush over her hair, but the spiky short hairs sprang back like barbed wire. She missed her long wild hair already and wondered how long it would take to grow.

"Sabine, how do I look?" Lalita presented herself in a red pantsuit.

"You look chic, Aunty." Sabine leaned on Lalita and inhaled the lavender aroma. It no longer gave her sneezing fits.

Their flights were leaving from Entebbe Airport, almost thirty-five kilometres from Kampala. It was only an hour's drive, but they had decided to leave early, having heard of military checkpoints on the way.

Sabine had an idea. "Aunty, we can leave in Bapa's lorry with our bags hidden behind the coffee sacks. The soldiers will think we're heading to the farm."

"Clever, clever Sabine!" Lalita patted Sabine's back.

They ate a light lunch of sandwiches and checked out of the hotel. Sabine carried her duffel bag outside, Bapa helped Lalita with her trunk, and Munchkin held on to Milo, his colouring book, and a box of crayons.

Sabine saw several people loading their bags onto their vehicles' roof racks. They, too, were headed for the airport. She recognized Mr. Singh, the owner of Bombay Silks, who had insulted Zena when they were shopping for fabric for their dance costumes. Next to him was a hunched old lady swaddled in a man's overcoat over a sari, presumably dressed for the chilly weather of Europe.

Soon Bapa pulled up in his lorry, the back filled with gunnysacks of coffee beans. He loaded their bags, making sure they were hidden behind the sacks. They squeezed together in the front seat and trundled south toward Entebbe.

As they left the outskirts of the city, Sabine saw fewer buildings and cars and more buses and boda-boda bicycles. Every cyclist carried a load strapped at the back: a bundle of wood or giant stalks of plantain or a sack of flour or coffee. What drew Sabine's breath away was a cyclist who braved the traffic with a tower of egg crates strapped onto his bike by rubber cords.

She began to count the eggs aloud. At least a thousand.

"They can work miracles," said Lalita in admiration.

The road ahead wound around green fields and warrens of mud and grass huts where women in bright kangas carried babies on their backs and loads on their heads.

12:00 noon. The news came on. "Today is day eighty-nine. All Indians who stay past the countdown will be sent to concentration camps in the north."

"Hasham Bapa," said Lalita sharply. "You can't stay here."

Bapa's snowy brow lifted as he exchanged a glance with Sabine. "Don't worry. I'm an African."

12:10 p.m. Airport Road stretched ahead, straight as an arrow. Munchkin coloured in his book, encouraged by Lalita's compliments. Sabine gazed out as Kampala, the city of seven hills, named after the pet impalas of the Buganda kings, faded into the distance.

The lorry jounced and jolted along the muddy terrain, and they came upon the rural savannah dotted with groves of eucalyptus trees. African totos, driving Ankole cattle with long, curvy horns, waved at them. Sabine waved back. In Kasenda, the birds would be singing and the coffee bushes covered with beans.

Lalita passed soda and groundnuts to everyone. Overhead, the sky stretched as blue as a robin's egg, and the morning sun was a ripe gold mango, split open, sweet and soft. Sabine swallowed. How could something so bad happen to Uganda, the Pearl of Africa? Would she ever be able to come back? Before she knew it, tears ran down her cheeks and she cried like a newborn baby. Lalita reached over to dry her tears, but Sabine saw that Lalita's eyes were wet as well. Bapa's, too. Silence reigned in the lorry, broken only by Munchkin's cries for more soda and groundnuts.

12:20 p.m. They screeched to a sudden stop at a make-shift barrier. A tree trunk rested on two oil drums. A twitch of fear fluttered in Sabine as she caught sight of a soldier leaning by the curb. Bapa got out. Sabine amused Munchkin by playing a hand game with him, keeping a close eye on Bapa chatting with the soldier. The soldier nodded, and Bapa gave him a carton of cigarettes and a thick envelope, probably bribe money, and returned to the lorry with a smile.

Bapa made two more stops. Each time it was a repeat of the earlier one: cigarettes and chai, and the soldiers waved them through.

1:30 p.m. The brakes squealed. Checkpoint again. Sabine saw a white 404 Peugeot, its luggage rack filled with bags, but there were no passengers inside. The soldiers came toward the lorry, leering at them.

"Muhindi. Toka nje! Get out!"

Bapa helped them climb down. Munchkin was so pleased to get out that he began to spin around like a wind-up toy, making gleeful noises. The soldiers clambered onto the back of the lorry. They found their bags and searched them with ruthless efficiency, filling their jute sacks with whatever they wanted. *Hurry, hurry.* Sabine wanted to get to the airport.

"Inspection. Line up!" shouted the soldiers.

They were rounded up like a herd of cattle about to be branded and led to a clearing. Several other Indian families were there already, their agony intensified by heat and flies. Among them were Mr. Singh and his old Ma, sweating rivers in her woolen overcoat.

An officer fired questions at them: "Why are you running away? Why are you so dressed up? How much money are you taking?"

Sabine whispered to Bapa, "They want us to leave, and we're leaving. Why are they delaying us and harassing us?"

"Beta, they've harboured years of repressed anger," Bapa whispered back. "First at the British, who played the role of white gods, then at us. Their rage is fizzing like a shaken soda bottle that has suddenly popped open. This is their last chance to punish us."

Mr. Singh stepped forward. "Good soldiers, let us go or we'll miss our flight."

"Shut up!" The officer slapped Mr. Singh, turned his pocket inside out, and left the white flap hanging. He checked the other pocket and found a ten-shilling note. "Eti, why do you keep money here?" He slipped the note into his own pocket and grinned.

The officer went to old Ma and pulled off her earrings and necklace. "You don't need these. You're going to a rich land." He yanked up her overcoat sleeve to check her arm and saw her thick gold bangle. He tried to pull it off.

The bangle moved a little but became stuck at her swollen, arthritic wrist. He pulled at it again. It didn't come off.

"Please, this is my wedding bangle," cried Ma. "I've worn it for fifty-five years."

The officer clapped, and immediately two of his cronies came running to him. They looked like young schoolboys. One of them had kind, espresso-hued eyes like Ssekore's. The officer barked orders, and the young soldiers joined the struggle, pulling at Ma's bangle.

Ma screamed in pain. The stubborn bangle held fast. The struggle continued.

The officer, now clearly angry, yelled, "Take the hand with the bangle."

Sabine's heart cramped. Ma's bloodcurdling scream rang in her ears.

Mr. Singh stepped forward. "Take me instead, sir, but stop troubling my Ma!"

"Trouble, eti. I'll show you what trouble is." The officer looked at his military cronies and said with a sinister smile, "Show him trouble."

The soldiers left Ma and grabbed Mr. Singh. They yanked at his jacket. A button popped off his coat and fell on the grass.

"Give him the bottle treatment!" yelled the grinning officer.

The young soldiers ran to Mr. Singh. They pulled off his turban, unravelling yards of red cloth. His hair was combed into a small bun on his head.

"Stop, you shameless people!" Ma screamed. But the

soldier grabbed Mr. Singh's hair while the second soldier picked up a broken beer bottle, cut across the strands of hair, and threw the thick black sheaf onto the grass.

"Stop! You beasts!" Ma thumped her fists on her chest.

The officer clapped, pointing to Ma, and the two soldiers returned to her.

"Wait!" cried Sabine. She looked at the young soldier who reminded her of Ssekore. "I can help. Please bring me some soap."

The young soldier looked at the officer for his consent.

"Go, fool. Didn't you hear? Get the soap," yelled the officer.

"Yes, Afande." The young soldier ran to a makeshift shed and promptly returned with a cake of blue Panga soap, which he gave to Sabine.

Sabine rolled up her sleeves, wet the soap with water from her water bottle to produce a slippery lather, and rubbed it gently on Ma's red wrist. Then she pulled and pulled at the bangle. It did not budge.

She rubbed the wet soap again, this time along the edges of the bangle, and then pulled at it again. It slipped off. The officer grabbed it immediately. Bapa dried Ma's hand with his handkerchief while Lalita blew air on the red, bruised hand to soothe the pain.

The officer shooed them off like cows back into their barn. "Go, go, go to India!"

They made their way quickly to their vehicles.

"You are a brave boy," said Ma, kissing Sabine's hand fervently and then pressing her hands on her head to crack her knuckles against her temples, a gesture to keep the evil eye away. "On the Day of Judgement their brains will spill out of their ears."

Lalita patted Ma's cheek. "Don't worry. We won't see them again."

The tearful Mr. Singh approached Sabine, his hands folded together into a prayer form. "Thank you, son," he said, bending down and touching Sabine's feet. "God bless."

When he rose, Sabine saw a tuft of black thread hanging from the torn button in his coat. They had stripped poor Mr. Singh of his dignity. She watched him leave, his arm hooked onto his old Ma. Sabine was glad to have been of help, and glad also that they had all thought she was a boy.

Bapa put his arm around her and Lalita put hers around Munchkin and they all returned to the lorry. "I'm proud of my little Simba," Bapa told Sabine.

3:00 p.m. The lorry bumped and rattled as it ran over potholes in the road, making them fly off their seats. With each jolt, Munchkin fell against Sabine, giggling. *Hurry, please.* She did not want to miss their flight. She began to count. Every minute that ticked by brought her closer to the airport. Strange! Now she was as determined to leave as she had earlier been to stay.

3:15 p.m. Checkpoint! Again!

"*Simama hapa!*" The soldiers waved their guns.

They got down and watched helplessly as the soldiers

rummaged through their bags. Sabine's eyes strained as the sun glared relentlessly at her. It, too, had joined hands with the oppressive military. The soldiers were angry. They grumbled that this was the last checkpoint, so they didn't get a good catch; the waters had been fished by others. The soldiers advanced toward them, leering. Sabine saw one soldier's face, three slashes across his burnished cheekbone, and stood transfixed. One-Eleven!

"Passports! Get your passports ready!" He clapped, grinning crookedly.

Everyone scrambled to retrieve documents from purses, pockets, and bags.

One-Eleven went to Bapa. "Where is your passport, mzee?"

"I'm *mwananchi*, a citizen," Bapa said in Swahili, showing his kipande.

"Eti, mzee, you passed the citizenship test?"

"Yes," said Bapa, and his chin rose.

"Good, good." One-Eleven smiled before moving on to Lalita.

Lalita held out her British passport. Ignoring it, he caught her fair arm, the one not in the cast. "Sister, how old are you?"

Lalita shrank back.

One-Eleven laughed the nasty laugh of the soldiers. "Eti, running away 'cause you don't want to marry a black man?"

He ruffled Munchkin's hair. Munchkin giggled. One-Eleven moved to Sabine.

"Your papers." The voice zapped like gunfire and the scars descended.

The scars were his, but they cut into Sabine like a razor. She heard him, smelled his smoky breath, saw his straggly black nasal hairs, but her hands were stiff as starch.

One-Eleven's gaze narrowed. "What are you staring at?"

Sabine looked helplessly at Bapa.

"Beta, show your papers to Afande," said Bapa.

One-Eleven drew closer to Sabine and scrutinized her as she reached into her pocket and retrieved the yellow folded refugee form. He straightened the form and studied it, frowning. Then he looked at her, his eye sunk in deep orbits. "You are a boy?"

"Yes, sir," she said at once.

He shook his head. "This document is forged." The words were hurled out with such force that they unsteadied her stance.

"No!" said Lalita.

"Don't argue," he said, wagging his finger at Lalita. He tapped at the photograph of Sabine that Bapa had hastily affixed on the form and gave her a reproachful stare. "Is this you?"

Sabine looked at the photo of herself with long hair and drew in her breath sharply. Her knees began to rattle.

One-Eleven tossed the form back at her. It hit her in the chest like a rock and dropped on the grass. Bapa picked it up. Behind her, she heard Munchkin whine and Lalita shushing to keep him quiet.

"Afande, the United Nations signed this document,"

said Bapa, his forehead shiny with sweat. "Where is the problem?"

"I say this document is forged." The virulent scars descended on Sabine again. "Are you a boy or a girl?"

She drew in her breath in convulsive gasps, a minnow caught in his hands. She nodded, then shook her head, then nodded again.

"Go in." He pointed to their makeshift office. "I want to check you."

Sabine's windpipe clamped. She saw One-Eleven's gun tucked into his holster and her neck muscles tightened. A bitter taste rose in her mouth. As if her mouth had a memory of its own, it brought back the time Butabika had raised her chin with his rifle. She could smell the gunpowder in One-Eleven's gun, feel it trickle into her throat and into her thudding chest. Her world went red and the drummer inside went berserk. *Dham, dham, dham. Dham, dham, dham.*

"Shoot me if you want, but I will not go inside," she said.

"Afande, she's my granddaughter," said Bapa. He clapped a hand on One-Eleven's shoulder and took him aside. They chatted in Swahili for what seemed like forever.

Finally Bapa came back. "Beta, quick, grab the wheel before he changes his mind. I cannot go with you." He placed the keys of his lorry in Sabine's hands; Lalita watched with an open mouth. He shook hands with Lalita, kissed Munchkin, and hugged Sabine. "I'll visit you when you're settled," he said, smiling.

Sabine nodded, taking Bapa's hand in hers, gripping it like a lifeline, afraid to let go. She looked at his cloudy eyes brimming with tears and felt she was drowning in them.

Slowly Bapa retrieved his hand. The cloudiness in his eyes parted and brightness shone as he stroked the letter *S* on her arm, laughing the way he always did. He gave her a gentle shove. "Go, please."

Every step away from Bapa tore into Sabine. Her feet turned impossibly heavy as gravity pulled at them as well. When she reached the lorry, she turned back, but Lalita caught her hand and led her firmly ahead.

Sabine sat at the wheel and pulled the driver's seat forward; her left foot pressed the clutch, and the right foot, the brake pedal. She turned the key and started the engine. She shifted gears. The engine coughed weakly, sputtered, and died.

"Ram, Ram!" Lalita cried, grabbing the dashboard. Munchkin giggled.

"Sorry!" said Sabine. She wiped her eyes and started again, pressing her shaky foot on the accelerator while engaging the clutch. The lorry lurched forward and moved slowly, away from the checkpoint, away from Bapa.

Ahead, the melting tarmac ran like a sticky black ribbon around the blue shores of Lake Victoria, empty except for a few boats and some caw-caw gulls. A torrent of sorrow pitched and rolled inside Sabine. *Goodbye, Bapa.*

4:35 p.m. She picked up speed. One thousand and one. One thousand and two. She counted the crawling seconds. Time ticked in her ears so loudly and yet so slowly.

— Going, Going, Going —

November 2, 1972

DAY 89

Entebbe Airport. Sabine's feelings churned inside her. Relief, regret, grief, and fear.

"Thank Ram!" Lalita cried, delirious with relief, kissing Munchkin and Sabine. Sabine put the keys under the driver's seat, as Bapa had instructed, and climbed into the back of the lorry to hand their bags to Lalita.

They joined their free hands together as they lugged their bags to the airport complex. Lalita's trunk was now almost empty. Sabine carried her much lighter duffel bag, and Munchkin his Milo.

An airplane taxied on the runway and took off.

"See that plane." Sabine showed Munchkin. "It's a big bus with wings. Do you want a ride in it?"

He looked at the plane with interest, then plugged his fingers into his ears to block out the thunderous roar.

At the entrance, a group of Africans waved placards at them that read *Go home.*

Inside, the terminal was a blur. Indian women in sweaters over glitzy saris took dainty steps as they pulled overdressed children or carried crying babies. At their sides, their husbands, instead of African porters, dragged unwieldy bags. Everywhere Sabine saw bewildered people staring into space, as if they were sleepwalking. Like her, they looked dazed by the thought of their unknown futures. Soon Uganda would be empty of Indians. Only a few loyal ones like Bapa would remain.

Sabine saw some soldiers lurking in a corner, smoking, and she quickened her stride. The soldiers must be flying as well. Papa had said the President rewarded his soldiers with "whiskey runs" by sending them on shopping sprees to London and Paris. Lalita's sharp eyes must have seen the soldiers, too, for she took Sabine's hand and tucked it into the crook of her arm. "Don't worry, dear. There are many of us to hide amongst."

They decided to check in their baggage and meet at the departure lounge. Lalita stood in a long line at the British Airways counter while Sabine took Munchkin to the Air France counter, where there was a long line as well. In these last few days, Sabine had stood in more lines than she had in her entire life before then.

5:20 p.m. The clock was a ticking time bomb. *Please hurry.*

She saw an African lady in a short, red leather skirt and red boots, escorted by two heavyset men, their shiny platform shoes squeaking, guns inside their holsters. Suits and guns did not go together. Suddenly Munchkin squirmed out of her grasp, waving Milo at … at … the lady.

Zena!

Sabine blinked. For a moment she thought she was hallucinating. Her heart turned into a bass drum. Her hands were soaked, and she felt her clammy fingers sticking to the handle of her duffel bag. Why was Zena here?

Zena ran to close up the distance between them, the two escorts trailing behind her.

She bent and kissed Munchkin. "You have become a big boy." She straightened and came closer. Sabine stepped back.

They looked at each other in disbelief. The silence was awkward.

A dizzying jumble of feelings—shock, awe, anger, concern—assaulted Sabine. She had waited a long time to get back at Zena, but now her voice shrivelled up. Her tongue, a strip of dry leather, lolled in her mouth. This was not the Zena Sabine knew. Zena's face was pasted with makeup, her hair coiled in tight cornrow plaits piled on top of her head. She looked ten years older. But beyond the makeup, Sabine saw Zena's kind eyes that had once laughed with her and shared secrets.

"Sabine, what happened to your hair?"

Sabine touched her head. Her hair stuck to her scalp with sweat and grime from her harrowing journey to reach the airport in time. She looked down to see her scruffy white shirt sticky and clinging to her skin. She was a mess. The air trapped inside her chest was painful. Finally she found her voice. "What are you doing here?"

"I'm flying to London," Zena said, pointing out the window.

Sabine saw a jet with the Uganda Airlines insignia parked on the runway. She supposed that as the Captain's niece Zena got free whiskey runs also.

Zena twisted her ring on her finger, and the diamond flashed. Her blackberry eyes sparkled like the diamond on her ring. "I'm going to marry Dada Amin."

Sabine felt the airport terminal rise and crash over her. Zena, her best friend, was going to be the President's wife! She recalled the strange news during the war days when the President got engaged to a young dancer. How could she? How could she marry the very man who was kicking Sabine's family out, who killed her uncle, who stole her life? How could she? Sabine didn't say anything.

"Are you leaving?"

"You are kicking us out, aren't you?"

Zena's face was pained. "Dada is trying to liberate our land."

"By grabbing our homes and shops."

They looked at each other, their silence now a plea for understanding. Zena raised her arm awkwardly, and Sabine saw the friendship bracelet on her wrist, the one she herself had made. Seeing it there told her that Zena still cared for her and had done what she could. Sabine felt a coolness settle on her forehead, slip into her throat and her heart. Her bitterness evaporated as well.

She hugged Zena. The worlds that separated them disappeared, and they became two childhood friends, twin beans of one coffee flower. They stood in the embrace for several seconds, whispering to each other.

"I'm sorry," murmured Zena. "Will you forgive me?"

Sabine nodded. "Please thank Uncle Asafa for helping Papa."

Zena nodded.

Sabine told Zena about Bapa stranded at the last check-point. Zena gestured to her bodyguards. She told them to call the army officer at the last checkpoint and release Mzee Hasham at once. She turned to Sabine.

"Please take good care of Bapa," Sabine managed to say.

"Your Bapa is my Bapa. I promise to look after him." Zena squeezed Sabine's arm. "Ssekore always asks about you."

Sabine flushed. "Tell him a special goodbye from me."

"I will miss you."

They hugged each other again, their foreheads pressed against each other, the moment sweet and sour, their tears mingling. Sabine didn't know if they were hers or Zena's.

"Quick-quick, there's no time to lose." Lalita grabbed Sabine's hand with one of her hands and took Munchkin's in her other, and they clung to each other, sweaty skins overpowered by lavender scents. Then, arms entwined, the three of them walked together to the departure gate like a six-legged airport creature.

Sabine noticed Lalita's fair arms, bare. "Aunty, your cast?"

"I gave my bangles to a poor child. No worries. With Ram's help I'll start over."

They stopped at the departure gate. The air felt too thick and charged to say anything. Lalita kissed Munchkin. "Be a good boy, na," she said, and she gave Sabine an affectionate hug, squeezing every bone in her body. Pressing a small idol of Ganesh, the god with the elephant head, into Sabine's hand, Lalita whispered, "For new beginnings." Then she pushed Sabine away gently, just as Bapa had.

The flight attendant led Sabine and Munchkin to their seats. All the seated passengers inside the plane were Indians. Munchkin began to play with his seatbelt, tightening and loosening it. Sabine put his tired head on her shoulder, and he dozed off.

The plane zoomed down the runway and then rose. Finally, she was leaving. Sabine felt a pang, but she also felt relief. Either way, staying or going, there was regret. She thought of a joke of Mama's that she hadn't understood at the time. *Life is a golden ladoo. If you eat the sweet, you will regret it. If you don't eat it, you will regret it.*

She pressed her nose against the cold window. Pinprick lights crowned the seven hills of Kampala at first, but soon she saw only darkness, aside from a single blinking light on the plane's wing. She took Uncle's model car out of her pocket. "Uncle, I'm taking you with me," she said quietly.

She thought about the future, her life in the new world. The best way to avenge the injustice, she decided, would be to live well and be happy. The tenacious gene of the dandelion in her would help her rise out of the African ashes and sow the seeds of a new Tree of Life.

In her mind, her eyes shifted right, left, right, left, to a count of eight beats, then reversed. Then her arms rose, sweeping forward and backward like a butterfly, spreading good will in all directions as in the dance of *shanta*, peace.

She felt herself grow lighter and lighter, as if she, too, were floating like the plane in the weightlessness of space outside. She felt her insides tingle and closed her eyes as Katana's song played in her mind. *O Mungu, O Mungu, Bless the child of dandelions.*

—— Historical Note ——

The first wave of Indian immigrants arrived in East Africa (Kenya, Uganda, and Tanzania) in the sixteenth century, when the rulers of East Africa, the Sultan of Zanzibar and the Portuguese colonials, recruited workers from the colony of Goa in India.

In the nineteenth century, the imperialistic European nations began the "Scramble for Africa." Britain acquired British East Africa (Kenya and Uganda), while Germany acquired German East Africa (Tanzania and other territories).

Subsequently the British colonials recruited more Indians from India to build the Kenya-Uganda Railway. In the six years it took Indian workers to construct the railway, hundreds died of malaria or other diseases or fell prey to the man-eating lions of Tsavo.

Upon completion of the railway in 1901, the Indians settled in East Africa. Some of them took up jobs in the government, others ran shops and became *dukawallas*—merchants—and a few, like my grandfather, became farmers.

The Indians in East Africa were a very diverse people. They were divided into distinct groups along religious lines—Hindu (like Lalita), Muslim (like Sabine's family), and Christian—and were further divided into different communities with origins in different regions or social classes in India. Members of each community had their own dress, food, culture, and dialect; their only commonality was their nutmeg skin and the country they or their ancestors were from. They were referred to as *wahindi* (or, in the singular form, *muhindi*)—Indians.

Within a short time, British East Africa grew prosperous. The British entrusted the trade and processing of their cash crops of coffee, tea, and sugar to the hands of the Indians, whom they considered more "efficient" than the Africans, paying no heed to the several tribal kingdoms headed by African chiefs.

Soon a class system was born. The British, or *wazungus*, owners of plantations, were first-class citizens; next came the Indians, middle-class traders; and finally there were the ethnic Africans, the *wananchi*, who did menial labour. Integration among the three groups was minimal.

In 1962 Uganda gained independence, with Mr. Milton Obote as Prime Minister and Sir Edward Mutesa, the Kabaka or King of the Buganda tribe, as President. Subsequently the British left Uganda, and the rift between the Indian minority and the African majority widened. A few years later, Mutesa was ousted and Obote appointed himself as the president.

Obote proclaimed the Common Man's Charter, which echoed the call for African socialism, or *ujama*, by Tanzania's President Julius Nyerere, who nationalized businesses and properties owned by Indians in Tanzania without compensation. On January 25, 1971, however, Obote was overthrown by his army chief of staff, Idi Amin.

Amin's power rested in the army, but it was deeply divided, and maintaining control was difficult as well as expensive. Amin's personal extravagance put an additional strain on the national budget. An easy answer to his pressing problem was to get rid of the Indians, who monopolized trade and commerce, and to redistribute their property. The "economic war of liberation" that he waged used the expulsion of Indians as a remedy for inequality. The nationalistic rhetoric was fueled by references to the Indians as foreign exploiters and as the "Jews of Africa," who must be "weeded out" so the *wananchi* could get back land that was rightfully theirs.

At that time, approximately 80,000 Indians lived in Uganda. About 60,000 of them had British passports; the remaining 20,000 were Ugandan citizens. During the ninety-day countdown of the expulsion of Indians in 1972, however, the military government did not make any distinction between Indians who were citizens of Uganda and Indians who were not.

In hindsight, one might say that the Indians were lucky to be expelled. Soon afterward there were gross human-rights violations and widespread killing. The Acholi and Langi tribal groups were persecuted for their loyalty to Obote. The government's security organization, the State Research Bureau, carried out torture and executions, killing church figures, lawyers, cabinet ministers, and anyone who opposed the regime, resulting in the deaths of between 300,000 and 500,000 Africans.

Amin's regime came to an end in 1979, when the Tanzanian army, backed by Ugandan exiles, responded to a Ugandan invasion by counterattacking. Amin escaped to

Saudi Arabia, where he, his six wives, and his twenty-five children were provided for until his recent death.

Today, peace reigns in Uganda. President Yoweri Museveni offered to compensate the expelled Indians and invited them to assist in the rehabilitation process. There is hope that in time Uganda will truly be the Pearl of Africa once more.

Acknowledgements

I am grateful to Margie Wolfe and Carolyn Jackson for their faith in the story and their editorial expertise and to Canada Council for the Arts for their kind support.

Thank you Kensington Writers and Martine Leavitt for your valuable feedback and encouragement.

Thank you to all the Ugandan exodees, who told me their stories.

This book would never have been a reality without my family's love and support. Astrum and Shaira—thank you for your many readings and candid critique. I wrote for you, not knowing that you would grow up faster than the book. Finally, my heartfelt thanks to my husband, Mohamed, who patiently read each draft so many times that he knows the story by heart.